RUGGERO VASARI

RAUN

TRANSLATED BY BRENDAN AND ANNA CONNELL
AND WITH AN INTRODUCTION BY
MARIA ELENA VERSARI

RAUN

RUGGERO VASARI (1898-1968) was an Italian poet and playwright and one of the founders of Italian Futurism. Among his works are the dystopian plays *L'angoscia delle macchine* (written 1923; published 1925) and *Raun* (written 1926-1927; published 1932).

BRENDAN and ANNA CONNELL have together translated numerous texts from Italian, including *Alcina and Other Stories* by Guido Gozzano (Snuggly Books, 2019).

MARIA ELENA VERSARI is Visiting Professor of Art History and Theory at Carnegie Mellon University. She studied at the Scuola Normale Superiore, where she received a PhD in Art History with a doctoral dissertation devoted to the international relations of Futurism in the 1920s. She has published numerous things, including two monographs, *Constantin Brancusi* (2005) and *Wassily Kandinsky e l'astrattismo* (2007), and edited the republication of Ruggero Vasari's Futurist dystopian dramas in *L'angoscia delle macchine e altre sintesi futuriste* (2009).

SNUGGLY BOOKS

TO THE COMRADES

FEDELE AZARI
GUIDO KELLER
SILVIO MIX

IN MEMORY

ISBN: 978-1-64525-107-1

CONTENTS

INTRODUCTION:

A MECHANICAL MYTHOLOGY

Myth, Necessity and Liberation

In his introduction to the first edition of *L'angoscia delle macchine* [tr. as "The Anguish of the Machines"] by his friend Ruggero Vasari, philosopher and critic Gino Gori reflected on what might be behind the impetus to put on stage a mechanized universe and to reveal its spiritual contradictions. He wrote: "Vasari's projects, especially *L'angoscia delle macchine*, have something in common with ancient myths, particularly the way they construct symbols which are virtually inherent to an image. This symbolization surmises a truth and then throws it into the tumultuous current of living things, as if it were an entity which does not belong to empirical reality, but rather to metaphysical reality." According to Gori, Vasari achieves this peculiar way of exploring the meaning of ideas, of making them act and react as if they were characters on a stage, by "thinking and conceiving in an irrational manner," by drawing from "that place beyond, in another world, where the thing-in-itself, the absolute, generates and manifests itself via a set of phenomena"(Gori 1925, xvi-xvii).

Vasari's poetic world, according to Gori, is populated by human figures who betray their own deepest identity as cosmic forces, as "universal types" of human experience and modes of thinking. These are, in the opinion of the expressionist writer Rudolf Kayser, the kind of characters who define a new form of drama, a drama which could go beyond the succession of actions justified by laws of causality or superficial psychological motivation (Kayser 1918, 119). In their theater, the Italian Futurists had already stressed the centrality of individual psychology. Vasari went beyond that by attempting to concretize an aspiration that, at that time, was fully felt in contemporary European circles. He created a theater in which action coincides with what Felix Emmel called the "visionary unveiling of irruptive human destiny" (Emmel 1924, 9) And this unveiling, or revelation, has something to do with the future of humanity and with its relationship to technology.

Already in his earlier collection of theatrical works, *La mascherata degli impotenti* [The Masquerade of the Impotent] (1923), Vasari had summarized the characters' individual identity, their appearance, with terse indications: "She, He…", or a few laconic personal names. These were "not defined personalities," but, to quote Gori again, "cosmic forces." They were forces which unceasingly ponder over their own roles, over their being part of a universal design which is both indecipherable and inalienable. This can happen "in whatever place," as Vasari himself lucidly points out. In *Sentimento*, for example, a man and a woman confront each other, both of them focused on searching for the deepest and irrational motivations behind their own self-annihilation. The uninterrupted contrast between submission and liberation, depravity and purity, create an unavoidable anguish, which imposes itself on the characters and overwhelms them. Their dense exchange reveals the forces that are overpowering them and at the same time their attempts, always frustrated, to free themselves from constraint by way of a catharsis of reasoning. The words excavate, reveal, and judge the irrational impulses that exist deep inside the characters' own identity, but they never really succeed in solving the contradiction of their irrational impulses, they never unfurl them in a rational way. Only a final eruption of violence, the elimination of both characters, will put an end to the drama.

One of the pieces included in *La mascherata degli impotenti*, *Il giustiziere* [The Executioner], had originally been titled *Anànke* - a title that reveals one of the conceptual fulcrums of Vasari's literary thought. In Greek mythology, Anànke is the female deity that oversees coercion, generates every compulsive action, and presides over every form of slavery and deep and incontrovertible bond, including that which arises from passion. It is also indicated by the name Necessity and, symptomatically, the bond it establishes between two individuals chains both to the roles defined by their relationship: slave and master, commander and commanded.

Indeed, the aspiration to understand and reveal the limits of human freedom and the inescapable relationship that binds man to destiny pervades the entirety of the Sicilian author's meditations. The thesis he wrote for his law degree, which he successfully defended in Rome in 1923, under the direction of the sociologist Enrico Ferri, is titled *I recidivi e l'idoneita' della pena* [Repeat Offenders and the Suitability of their Punishment]. Another thesis, which had been rejected by the Turin degree commission two years earlier, because it was judged indecent, investigated *La personalità della prostitute* [The Personality of the Prostitute]. Even as a law student, Vasari was interested in discovering what drives human beings to act in a certain way, and to constantly repeat the same behavior. Or to translate this into the language of theater, one could ask: what makes a character a "universal type"? Beginning in the mid-nineteenth century, European culture struggled in its search for a code to decipher individual identity and classify it into ancestral models of behavior. Literary culture and scientific culture were joined in this research, which led to the creation of several new areas of study. Cesare Lombroso codified criminal anthropology and, in 1893, published a volume of great impact, *La donna delinquente, la prostituta e la donna normale* [The Criminal Woman, the Prostitute and the Normal Woman], in which he interpreted prostitution as an atavistic residue of prehistoric behavior. In these investigations, physiological conformation, psychological identity and criminal propensity overlapped. Enrico Ferri, Lombroso's student, even went so far as to deny the existence of free will, writing "if man had free will, more or less independent from determining causes, it would no longer be possible to conceive the same personality, as a permanent aspect of the individual character" (Ferri 1900, 490). And "personality" is, for Ferri and for Vasari as well, the inner energy that each individual has in order to develop in an (predetermined) individual way.

From the inevitability of individual human destiny, as Gino Gori writes in his *Il grottesco nell'arte e nella letteratura* [The Grotesque in Art and Literature], derives "a struggle between what is and what destroys, between one *individuality* and other, opposing and hostile individualities." This struggle, as we have seen, is at the center of a new model of tragic theater based on the clash of archetypal forms. "If this is a metaphysical speculation that is artistically realized in exemplifying images," Gori states, "the tragic character can only be a typical sort that is however not traditional. [...] In the new meaning that I intend to give to it, the type is a synthesis of synthesis, a synthesis heightened in power" (Gori 1927, 105). Subject to the imperative imposed on them by their own "personality," Vasari's characters are inevitably forced to reveal themselves as "absolute types," and fully become what they already are *in nuce*. In *Il giustiziere*, for example, the character of the father witnesses his daughter's depravity and, confronted with the acknowledgement of inevitability, says: "Go! Go! Run, my daughter, to your joy! Carry out your mission of destruction! Without blood, without prostitution, the world dies."

In those same years, Expressionists and Futurists saw the prostitute as the idol of a new fringe aesthetics aimed at linking anti-bourgeois feelings with the celebration of new icons, created by the modernity of the metropolis. The anarchic desire for the destruction of traditional values cohabits with the stigmatization of the figure of the *femme fatale*, who, for Marinetti, embodied the instinct to crush and annihilate male creative energies. While adapting both of these concepts in his work, Vasari distanced himself from the ideology of Marinetti, making the inevitable contrast between man and woman the source of the disintegration of the new mechanical ideology.

For Vasari, the prostitute was both a muse for the man of genius and a bringer of death. In *Raun* (1932), he writes: "The prostitute embodies the dangerous life - it's bravery that is paid for with blood [...] - it's feverish sterility - the inviolate womb - it's demolition. Only the creator can feel for this kind of female [...]." The Great Prostitute Sacar indeed channels the creative capacities of its subjects which, possibly recalling Sigmund Freud, Vasari identifies as coming from a sublimated sexual aspiration. But the atavistic force that she exercises over Volan and over all the inhabitants of Raun also becomes the most effective tool for universal enslavement used by the Red Man in his dictatorship. In this universe, sensuality and mechanicity merge, held together by the icon of Sacar, which Volan calls "the animal joy of our mechanical joy."

In the *Manifesto dell'arte meccanica* [Manifesto of Mechanical Art] (1923), Ivo Pannaggi, Vinicio Paladini and Enrico Prampolini had foreseen the advent of a similar modern universe which would celebrate the new man as a creator under the auspices of the machine: "Today the Machine marks the rhythm of the great collective soul and of the various individual creators. The Machine chants the Song of the Genius. The Machine is the new divinity which illuminates, dominates, distributes its gifts and punishments in this futurist time of ours, which is devoted to the great Religion of the New" (Prampolini, Pannaggi, Paladini 1923, 2) Progress in this mechanical age underscores the idea of a linear development of universal history. But this final psychological re-determination, which should take place within the historical conscience of the modern man or woman, is helpless against the return of the atavistic categories which chain each individual to his or her particular "type." The work of Vasari thus stages the clash between the desire for power and the action of the modern superman ("VOLAN — Life is action - action either creates or destroys. / SILLAN — Without any purpose? / VOLAN — It doesn't matter. To live is to act - the desire to be.") and the resurfacing of the atavistic identity of the individual, chained to the fatal consequences of his or her own personality. Echoing Schopenhauer and Nietzsche, Vasari reflects on the myth of the eternal return and sees in the extreme typification of individuals the root of a never-ending identical repetition of situations which have already occurred. "So it happens that," citing Gori once more, "what I now am I was already, what I was, I will be for the whole of Time, an infinite number of times, as a toy of the obscure and incomprehensible Will, without motive, which is the hidden spring deep inside the elements" (Gori 1927, 108). And yet, surprisingly, by giving power to this fixity of destiny, Vasari is able to stimulate the atavistic layer of his characters with the dynamics of the present. This continuous working of opposing forces brings a definite collapse to the completely voluntary, and therefore unstable, equilibrium on which the realm of machines is based.

As Nietzsche taught in the second essay of his *Untimely Meditations,* life is action and life is forgetting, and, it is precisely through the reemergence of a memory, which is both personal and ancestral, that the characters of *Raun* gradually abandon the faith in the abstract vitality of the machine, the new futurist divinity.

In Vasari's texts, it is the female character who always suggests an opening towards the remote past, the oblivion of which is a necessity for the abandonment of any remaining humanity, or a remote past that resurfaces as a projection of a previous existence, without the characters being fully aware of it ("VOLAN — In the stream of my consciousness men and deeds still wander - enveloped in a thick fog … […] / SILLAN — Everything repeats itself.") The past reemerges and is projected onto a mechanistic present, creating a burst of violence and death.

Science Fiction's Mythical Horizon, Millenarianism and Utopia

Vasari's pessimism vis-à-vis the Futurists' myth of the machine did not fail to elicit Marinetti's criticism. As a result, Vasari carried out a more decisive ideological and political rupture with the Futurist leader. In a private letter, he criticized Marinetti's vision of the machine as steeped in a languid, sensual and regressive rhetoric. Compared to his previous works, in *Raun,* he offered a more systematic, sociological analysis of the form of dystopia offered by the reign of the machines.

Vasari describes the behavior of the masses of *Raun* and the psychological conditioning that accompanies it in a much less stereotyped way. The agitation of the crowd of Ergons, disappointed by the fact that construction of the tower has been interrupted, manifests itself on several occasions and even takes on a voice of its own in Ergon I's pleas to Volan. As a testimony to the ideology adopted by the masses, but also of the means used to achieve their adherence, Vasari stages a veritable battle of persuasive oratory. Volan's argument ("You are no longer machines! The passions which have been crushed inside this tangle of gears - pulverized by the arrogance of the power hammer - stunned by the sharp teeth of electricity - have not been totally annihilated. So you have become human again.") is countered by Sillan's ("Volan is bewitching you all - he is pushing you towards suicide! He tells you: destroy the world you have created with your own hands").

The entire play is strewn with exhortations, reasoning and courtly celebrations which place at the forefront of the stage the linguistic hypertrophy of the propaganda of the mechanical utopia, as well as that of the counter-utopia of the renegade prophet Volan. Particularly effective in this regard are the brief cheers with which the choir welcomes each of the young women directed by the Ginemachine to each of the three possible female social roles. Completely contradictory to each other and comically antithetical, these short panegyrics are perfect examples of a rhetoric of propagandistic conditioning. Vasari acutely intersperses them in the dispute between Sacar and Ber, which reveals the less noble detail that the Ginemachine's selections are in fact manipulated to guarantee the interests of the State. The passage contains constant references to the "wearing," "replacement," "reduction of years of service," and the "end in the blast furnaces" of the human material that constitutes the workforce, offering an effective counterpoint to the choir's celebratory litanies.

As pointed out by Niccolò Sigillino in the introduction to the first edition of *Raun*, "the triumph of anti-spiritual automaton over the feeling individual, is, then, the triumph of mechanical civilization over bourgeois civilization." This staged conflict between opposite visions of the world is also a palimpsest of registers and literary styles: "the fantastic, the mimic, the tragic, the epic, and also the grotesque act on the same plane, in a kind of profane apocalypse" (Sigillino1932, 7).

The spectacular stage design that Vasari had conceived for *Raun*, revealed by the detailed technical instructions inserted in the text, further clarifies his desire to modulate the drama through this hypertrophy of images and words that arouse both attraction and repulsion in the reader and in the audience. The tower of Raun, with its glass booth for the director of the works, is inspired by the tower that Tatlin designed ten years earlier as a monument to Lenin; the scene of the Ginemachine, with the choir members seated on continuously rotating cylinders of various heights, anticipates future scenographic solutions by over fifty years. And it is precisely this fascination for the visual (and visionary) apparatus of the realm of machines that establishes Vasari's dramas as fully belonging to the Futurist tradition.

The myth of a new aesthetic harmony established by machines, recognized and celebrated by the Futurists, was in the 1920s and 1930s (and probably still is today) a central element for any possible discussion of modernity and contemporary civilization. Aware of this fact, Vasari rejected the accusation of having created a theater that merely staged a debate between abstract models of philosophical concepts. In an unpublished letter to the Polish writer Jalu Kurek, he wrote: "The eternal problems of the individual are always the same, but they should always be felt in relation to their own time. So my Tonchir can be Prometheus, as wells as Faust. But he doesn't live in either a myth or metaphysics—he lives now, in the midst of machines."

Vasari does not deny the aesthetic appeal of the new technocracy; on the contrary, he makes it the core from which the fascination of his theatrical performances derives. It is for this reason that his stage directions are so detailed. In his correspondence with his European colleagues, he often repeats how important it is that his texts be set to Futurist music, such as that of Silvio Mix and Luigi Russolo's *intonarumori*. It is only through a holistic aesthetic experience that the dictatorial world of machines can be lived and understood. Perfection and harmony are the codes that the Red Man declares as the supreme values of the empire of Raun and in which the individuality of each inhabitant is dissolved: "Each individual is a cog in this great machine - in this absolute perfection of life. We have found the source of true happiness. […] All is order - discipline. The machine - our divine and adored creature - has taught us perseverance - moderation - precision. We do not want anything else. For this civilization - for this per-fection - for this harmony of life - we wanted to erect the greatest monument - to which we have sacrificed everything."

Facing this voluntaristic and totalizing harmony, the palingenetic dream of Vasari's heroes reveals an in-ner contrast between utopian and messianic models. In *Raun*, Volan rises up as the true and real Antichrist of the kingdom of machines, as a force working against it from within. After his sudden conversion, that is, after having lost faith in the power of human thought and faced with the error of his own calculations, he gives up the project of the tower to turn his attention "down below - where men suffer." But his new mission is also defined by the story of his alter ego, an architect who lived in Ancient Rome, Aterius. Appearing as a ghostly projection of Volan's subconscious mind, Alterius reveals the eternal recurrence of his (and Volan's) relation with Sacar, muse and vampire at the same time ("ARCHITECT — You are the diverter - you are diverting all of humanity"). Vasari superimposes and mixes a large number of cultural references that allow us to understand the new role assumed by Volan. There is no shortage of Christological references, while the story of Volan's relationship with the virgin Saib, with whom he conceives a son by breaking the sacred laws of Raun, openly follows the foundation myth of Rome.

In his *History of Utopia*, Jean Servier wrote that "if utopia is a closed city, millennialism is a storm that must wash humanity of its sins according to God's will and give the inheritance of the riches of the earth to the conspiratorial brotherhood" (Servier 1967, 357). Still, the escape from Raun and the destruction of the city of the machines do not lead to the long-awaited perfect conclusion in the Eden of Nature. Vasari's irony follows men, bewildered, nostalgic, to a deserted island inhabited by ferocious beasts. Passion awakens between a young man and a young woman, according to the codes that distinguish the stereotyping of sexual roles. As in *L'angoscia delle macchine*, the final scene ends with the mouths of men kissing the earth, which has again taken on the role of the Great Mother, after having ousted the divinity of the Machine sung by the Futurists. Emotions once more guide and enliven human existence, but in the background a question remains: how long can this human identity, freed from the strength of will, resist the temptation of machines and of a new submission ("MAN IV. — Save the machines! Without them, we would have never been able to come here! [...] MAN VI. — Free us from all temptations! Destroy them! [...] MAN IX. — (*speaking through the megaphone*) Men - on your knees! This is your liberation!").

—Maria Elena Versari

The present essay is a shortened version of that which was published in Ruggero Vasari, *L'Angoscia delle macchine e altre sintesi futuriste*, ed. by Maria Elena Versari, Palermo: Due Punti 2009.

Works cited:

Felix Emmel, *Das ekstatische Theater*, Prien: Kampmann & Schnabel Verlag 1924.

Enrico Ferri, *Sociologia criminale*, Turin: Fratelli Bocca editori, 1900.

Gino Gori, "Introduzione," in Vasari 1925.

Gino Gori, Il grottesco nell'arte e nella letteratura, Rome: Alberto Stock 1927.

Rudolf Kayser, "Das Neue Drama," in *Das junge Deutchland*, I, n. 5, 1918.

Jean Servier, *Histoire de l'utopie*, Paris: Gallimard 1967.

Niccolò Sigillino, "Il teatro di Ruggero Vasari," in Vasari 1932.

Ruggero Vasari, *La mascherata degli impotenti e altre sintesi teatrali*, Rome: Edizioni "Noi" 1923.

Ruggero Vasari, *L'Angoscia delle Macchine. Sintesi tragica in tre tempi*, Turin: Edizioni Rinascimento 1925.

Ruggero Vasari, *Raun. L'uomo e la macchina*, Milan: Casa editrice "La Lanterna" 1932.

TRANSLATORS' NOTE

The present translation of *Raun* was made from the 1932 edition published by La Lanterna, in Milan. As with most Futurist authors, Vasari uses idiosyncratic punctuation. We have retained this, despite the fact that it occassionally, such as in the lack of comas, gives odd readings. In the original text there is also sometimes a lack of consistency with capitalization, punctuation, etc. Again, we have opted to present the text as it is in Italian, rather than "cleaning it up" for its English version. There are many cases where we have been tempted to add footnotes, but have chosen to present the text without these, as such sidetracks, it is felt, would interfere with the peculiar music of the play.

The "Plot for Cinematography" is present in the edition that we worked with and is therefore included here. Though it generally follows the plot of the text of the play, it does not do so exactly. It also adds insight into many aspects of the play, and is thus an important document in its own right.

RAUN

CHARACTERS

THE RED MAN
SACAR
VOLAN
SILLAN
SAIB
ARCHITECT
GIRL
YOUNG MAN
BER
MAN-NUMBER
CAPTAIN
TWO AIR MECHANICS
LOUDSPEAKER

CHORUS - ERGONS - INITIATES
VIRGINS OF RAUN - MEN

The action takes place in Raun, Metropolis of the Future Era of Machines

The workers of Raun,
who are without sexual distinction, are called "ergons";
"initiates" are the intellectual element

I.

THE TOWER OF RAUN

SCENE: *The tower of Raun rises. On top of mighty iron shelves, two circular scaffoldings are built, one above the other. To the left and to the right, wedged between the scaffoldings, are elevators in motion. On the lower scaffolding is a glass booth. It is the directorate of works: high tables, which are like lecterns, are covered with plans and drawings. Loudspeakers. Television equipment. Electric bells. Volan and Sillan are studying plans and making calculations. On the scaffolding above, which is partially taken up by materials, machines and tools, the ergons, furnished with breathing masks, are working. The top of the tower is enveloped in fog.*
DOMINANT ATMOSPHERE: lead-grey with silver reflections.

ERGON I. — The fog is bothering my nose.
ERGON II. — Then cut it off! One useless thing the less.

ERGON I. — Right - I wouldn't feel pain - it's numb.

ERGON III. — You'll feel the cold - higher up!

ERGON I. — Aren't we high enough?

ERGON III. — To me it seems that we're just getting started.

ERGON II. — Up you go. You have to touch the heavens.

ERGON I. — What do you mean by heavens?

ERGON II. — When one can no longer breathe.

ERGON I. — Then we're in the heavens!

ERGON II. — The sun isn't showing itself.

ERGON III. — The sun is old - at night it can't sleep - in the morning it rises late - it hasn't opened the windows yet.

ERGON I. — If this fog doesn't clear - it's going to go right into my brain!

ERGON III. — This sun is old. It's been reduced to poverty - it's ended up in a rented room - without heat.

(*On a panel inside the glass booth, the number 9100 lights up in red*).

VOLAN — (*absorbed in analysis*) — Nine thousand one hundred…

SILLAN — (*with joy*) 9100 meters high!

VOLAN — Reached.

SILLAN — The tower is climbing into the heavens.

VOLAN — No one is higher than us.

SILLAN — Seeing the whole earth at our feet.

VOLAN — Going up - up - and when will you ever come down?

SILLAN — Joy of returning amongst the living.

VOLAN — Thought lives up high - the senses live below.

SILLAN — But you are also living - and Sacar the female lives too.

VOLAN — Sacar is flesh.

SILLAN — Sacar will adorn herself with the most beautiful jewel. One that was not born from the womb of the earth - but sprang from the brain of Volan. The Tower of Raun is the jewel of Sacar.

VOLAN — I'm building the tower to tell the Initiates: try to exceed me! - and to tell Raun: it's Volan's will!

SILLAN — To tell Sacar: I have beat your master!

VOLAN — The Red Man is the despot - the despot over all.

LOADSPEAKER: Glory to you - Volan - who has forged billions and billions of metallic arms to seize the sky. Never before have the centuries seen such a marvel - never has a human genius so dared. Honor to you - Volan - the era of machines will sing your name.

VOLAN — My tomb shall be here!

SILLAN — Above - the first light for you!

(*The luminous panel shows the number: 9101*)

VOLAN — 9101.

SILLAN — Sacar will kiss your forehead when you get to ten thousand meters - when the great work has been completed.

VOLAN — My mind is not on Sacar - the tower is on my mind.

SILLAN — When the craving for gold no longer exists - because you have everything - when the craving for power no longer exists - because you are everything - the female shall be able to say: create for me.

VOLAN — Yes - when the female can no longer contaminate this beauty with her embrace.

SILLAN — And so?

VOLAN — Life is action - action either creates or destroys.

SILLAN — Without any purpose?

VOLAN — It doesn't matter. To live is to act - the desire to be.

SILLAN — Are we repudiating the idea of the life of the past?

VOLAN — We're modifying it. (*pause*) In the stream of my consciousness men and deeds still wander - enveloped in a thick fog...

SILLAN — So?

VOLAN — An architect - in which Roman period? - a temple - a female - in the destiny of a man there is always a female - is this really true? - a violent death...

SILLAN — Everything repeats itself.

ERGON III. — The shuttle of the elevators are weaving the tower.

ERGON II. — Cast into space - our arms are giant cranes lifting up mountains.

ERGON III. — The mountains do not touch the sky.

ERGON I. — We are fraying the clouds.

ERGON II. — When will there ever be peace for us?

ERGON I. — Peace? Then is work not peace for you?

ERGON II. — When I know what I want.

ERGON I. — Want? You don't have to want anything - you have to work - either here - or in the mines - or in the workshops - or on the flying machines - wherever - everywhere - you have to act.

ERGON II. — I am searching for peace.

ERGON III. — Peace? How pitiful!

ERGON I. — Who are you envious of?

ERGON II. — Our masters who have the females.

ERGON I. — The female does not bring peace.

ERGON III. — Do you know the anguish and torments of being?

ERGON II. — No. I am a cog wheel that bites another wheel.

ERGON I. — It's them - our masters - who give you this wheel to bite - a wheel that you would otherwise never know how to find.

(*An electric alarm sounds with a roar*)

VOLAN — An earthquake?

SILLAN — The seismographer is measuring a level four magnitude.

VOLAN — And yet it doesn't seem like it - the ground didn't shake.

SILLAN — (*surprised*) What do you mean?

VOLAN — (*he is carefully checking a few seismic instruments, and then he closes his eyes*) Now - I understand…

SILLAN — A miscalculation - in the laying of the foundations?

VOLAN — I am going to interrupt the work. (*he touches a button. The sound of a bell. On the upper scaffolding a red light flashes: "Stop!" Immediately the Ergons cease working. He speaks into a device)* Everyone down!

SILLAN — Everything has stopped.

VOLAN — Yes.

SILLAN — Did you look? - examine?

VOLAN — It's useless to look.

SILLAN — The Red Man?

VOLAN — I will take full responsibility.

(*Pause*).

SILLAN — You're upset - you think…

VOLAN — I am thinking about myself - about being unable to proceed further!

(*The Ergons are coming down in the elevators*).

SILLAN — They're coming down.

VOLAN — I ordered it.

SILLAN — So, you are quitting…

VOLAN — I'm not quitting. (*examining several diagrams*). Look - all the calculations are accurate - check - and yet the tower is giving in - at 7000 the trestles have bent - they won't be able to support the immense weight for long - then the mountain of iron will collapse…

SILLAN — Then we are going to need to demolish from the top down to 7000 - reinforcing from 5500 - we can then rebuild to 10,000 - it will take a lot of effort - but we'll prevail…

VOLAN — Words.

SILLAN — Calculations.

VOLAN — Words.

SILLAN — Millions of Ergons will lend you their arms - millions of Ergons await - they are kneeling in front of the miracle of the era of machines...

VOLAN — What can strength do - what can the will do - when there is no brain regulating this strength - this willpower?

SILLAN — The failure of science? - The death of thought?

VOLAN — The destruction of the infinity of thought - affection - faith - will – future... I acknowledge the uselessness of thought...

SILLAN — You are revealing horrible things to me.

VOLAN — I'm not revealing anything to you - it is this tower which is revealing...
(*he climbs to the upper scaffolding*).

SILLAN — (*sits down deeply distressed*).

VOLAN — The tower abandoned - life has stopped up here - my life also has come to a halt - now the descent - to descend - emptiness - the void - to cast oneself into the void... (*Pause*) I don't want to witness the distruction of my strength!... O space - swallow me up! (*Locked inside his own anguish, his one desire being to die, he collapses. After a few moment he snaps up as if struck by a vision. His expression is one of great bewilderment. The man has been transfigured*).

LOUDSPEAKER — Sacar is coming up the tower.

SILLAN — (*panicking*) Danger! The tower is collapsing!

VOLAN — My word that has condemned man - now will save him. (*Pause*) I erected the tower because my vanity coveted the unreachable - now I shall demolish it because my humility doesn't want me here - higher than everyone - but down below - where men suffer - where men have invented machines to destroy bit by bit the spirit - the soul...

SACAR — (*exiting the elevator, with anxiety*) What's happening? The tower... Where is Volan?

SILLAN — He's up there... he knows... (*Both climb to the upper scaffolding*).

SACAR — Volan!

VOLAN — You are in danger - Sacar - the tower might collapse...

SACAR — (*ruefully*) The tower - was for me...

SILLAN — It shall always be - we will stop the threat.

SACAR — Volan is discouraged - the dangerous prey has slipped from his grip of steel - now he is suffering. (*Pause*) Leave us alone - I need to know everything - my tenderness will loosen the grip of the claws that are torturing his soul.

SILLAN — (*makes as if to leave*).

VOLAN — Comrade - where are you going? Sacar the female - the animal joy of our mechanical joy - the soft smile within the sharp smile of the machines - Sacar - this malleable machine of pleasure - is coming - to me - because she sees the tower disappearing - the tower erected by the Red Man in her honor - she is coming - to me - to beg me...

SILLAN — (*making as if to put his hand over Volan's mouth*) Your lips are uttering blasphemies!

SACAR — A thick fog - black as a tropical night - has covered his mind.

VOLAN — Never before has my mind seen such light - it is dazzled by the light.

SACAR —Sillan - go! I will face the scorn of this visionary alone!

SILLAN — He's crazy!

VOLAN — I'm not crazy - you're ungrateful!

SILLAN — I no longer see in you my teacher.

LOUDSPEAKER — The Ergons are rioting - they are angered at having to abandon the tower.

SACAR — The tower is also their work - their entire soul - they have put all their energy into it.

SILLAN — I'll run to calm them (*he goes down*). (*Yelling from the Ergons*).

SACAR — The Ergons are crying your name - you should not face them. At a signal from the Red Man they will crush you...

VOLAN — No one will touch me.

SACAR — (*gently*) I've lived only for you. The one name in me: Volan - a dream in me: the tower - do you understand me?

VOLAN — Yes.

SACAR — You understand? You listened?

VOLAN — Yes.

SACAR — Now - the threatening tower - years and years of work - only you can save it - and you step back...

VOLAN — I cannot...

SACAR — So you have built in order to destroy - is this your vengeance?

VOLAN — You are mistaken.

SACAR – Isn't there any longer any joy of life in you? And if I were to give you my lips - my lips which the entire empire of Raun bows to?

VOLAN — Your lips belong to the Red Man.

SACAR — They will be yours - for you only - but... the tower...

VOLAN — You - the Queen of Raun - the Red Man's woman - Sacar the female - the one who nobody has ever been able to look at without their eyes lighting up with desire - you want to offer me your lips - but - in exchange - you ask me for the tower...

SACAR — (*annoyed*) You built it so you could have me. The tower was supposed to be your triumph - you built it to annihilate the Red Man - to steal his woman...

VOLAN — My only wish was for the tower to make people remember you in the centuries to come. Every creator needs an inspiration. I have transfused your beauty and your power into this masterpiece. You were the Great Prostitute - you were my inspiration. The prostitute is the dangerous life - it's bravery that is paid for with blood - it's a mouth impregnated with the smell of other males - understanding how to kiss like a virgin - and many times she imprints on one's lips the blood of another man - it's feverish sterility - the inviolate womb - it's demolition. Only the creator can feel for this kind of female - in his mad dream he grabs hold of her with a spasm - and thus she gives equilibrium to the potential of his being. But this female is a phantom… and she must remain a phantom forever.

SACAR — I saw you - Volan - master of Raun - going through the Metropolis - and I saw a female following your steps…

VOLAN — Being a master is no longer for me.

SACAR — You must always be a master - I want to live - you must let me live.

VOLAN — Too late! My life is not that…

SACAR — I was distant from you - because I was too taken with you. But now I have come and will tell you: here I am - erect the tower - let us live. You despise me - destroy this last hope of mine - this desire of mine - which is enormous and devours me completely - you smash it into pieces. Draw away your fears! You lived for the sake of love - you built for the sake of love - you became a god for the sake of love. Love is now reaching out to you - but you are humiliating it. Stop the tower from collapsing - keep building it up - let it be alive the same way it was alive in your self.
(*From the elevators, a crowd of Ergons pour out onto the lower scaffolding. They are agitated. A sordid anger seems to be exploding. Threatening gestures. Whining.*)

ERGON I. — Let's get back to work - now!

ERGON II. — The tower is our blood!

ERGON I. — We will never abandon the tower.

ERGON III. — Volan will punish us!

ERGON II. — It's our work!

ERGON I. — We are not moving from here!

ERGON III. — Sillan wants the tower!

ERGON II. — Let's get going - Sillan will lead us.

SACAR — The Ergons are coming up - they are angry!

VOLAN — I will order the demolition now.

SACAR — I will never allow it!

VOLAN — The Ergons have to obey me!

ERGON I. — Let's all go to Volan.

ERGON II. — Yes - everybody!

ERGON III. — *(to I.)* You will talk for us.

ERGON II. — Volan can order that we all shall be killed - more of our comrades will come…
(They climb to the upper scaffolding. As they climb, other Ergons take over the lower scaffolding).

ERGON I. — Grand Master - we have all gathered here to beg you to save the tower. You were the one who wanted this tower to be built - so that no human eye could ever see the very top of it. The machines never had a chance to rest - the Ergons competed with the machines to supply you with materials - which the belly of this monster sucked down - without ever being satiated. All of our life is here - don't destroy the tower - a whole era is being glorified.

VOLAN — Nobody will ever be able to save the tower.

ERGON I. — You are the only one who can. It's your creature - you nailed your entire life to a desk in order to make calculations for it. You are the only one. Even if we were all to die - Raun will give you more arms.

SACAR — The marvel of the era of machines! For the very first time the whole earth is one man with one will! Are you still able to give up?

VOLAN — It's not me who is giving up. There is somebody who wants to destroy the tower in order to save this humanity which doesn't have anything human left in it - this humanity which is blinded by pride and power - this humanity which has forgotten about feelings - love - compassion. I have but one command: demolish the tower! Obey me and you will be saved!
(*Movement from within the crowd. Sillan suddenly appears*)

SILLAN — Volan is deceiving you! He is betraying your work! For years you have been wearing yourself out. Now he tells you to demolish the tower - you need to cry out: the tower is ours!

ERGONS — The tower is ours! - The tower is ours!

SILLAN — Volan has been my teacher - I'm the only one who is aware of his plans. He built the tower in order that - once it reached this height - it would collapse. He deceived you. His calculations were correct - more than correct in order to make the tower collapse. He hates all of you - he hates the Red Man - our despot - he hates Sacar - the powerful one among the powerful ones - he hates our empire - he wants to ruin everything. Does the era of machines need him as its destroyer?

VOLAN — Sillan - my disciple?

SACAR — Defend yourself! Don't challenge the holy anger of the Ergons!

VOICES — To death! Throw him off the tower! He has betrayed us!

(*The crowd surges. Fists tighten.*)

VOLAN — Your cries are a delight to my soul - humanity is waking up in you - you are no longer machines! The passions which have been crushed inside this tangle of gears - pulverized by the arrogance of the power hammer - stunned by the sharp teeth of electricity - have not been totally annihilated. So you have become human again. Feelings have arisen in you once more. You want blood! Passion is blood! (*pause*). But if my blood could melt the metal foil in which your hearts are encased - here I am: kill me!

(*A moment of confusion among the crowd*).

SILLAN — Volan is bewitching you all - he is pushing you toward suicide! He tells you: destroy the world you have created with your own hands - disappear from the earth - nothing more is left for you. What impotence! What abnegation! The era of machines does not permit a return to the past - it does not permit pause. We have mechanized the world for the joy of the living. Machines have given you everything. Free yourself from the weight of the soul - you will live without torments. Suppress anybody who wishes to push you into nothingness!

VOLAN — (*to Sillan*) — Do you really want my head?

SILLAN — I want to build the tower.

VOLAN — You will not succeed! You only want to build yourself up above me.

SILLAN — I will rebuild the tower!

VOICES — We want the tower! Viva Sillan!

SILLAN — Throw him off! His death will save the civilization of machines!

VOICES — Off! Off! We want to live!

ERGONS — (*They grab Volan and drag him onto the edge of the scaffolding*)

SACAR — Don't touch Volan. Volan is still your leader. None of you can judge him. The Red Man will give his judgment.

(*Movement of the crowd*)

LOUDSPEAKER — The Red Man - the purest heir of our mechanized race - will come and pass judgment. Men on the tower - men on the earth - his word is law! (*The crowd gathers religiously. The Red Man comes out of the elevator onto the upper scaffolding. Everyone prostrates at his feet. The scene darkens in order to emphasize, with spotlights, the figure of the Red Man.*)

THE RED MAN — For the very first time in my empire discipline has been broken. Initiates and Ergons have been overcome by passions - they appoint themselves as judges. Whoever - whoever was the first - to go back to the tower - the first to have disobeyed Volan - must pay for his disobedience with his life!

ERGON I. — (*coming forward*) It was I!

THE RED MAN — Cast him into the void!

ERGON I. — Long live the civilization of machines! Receive me - O space - into your soft embrace - give me a beautiful death! Long live the Tower of Raun! (*he jumps into the void. By means of a steel cable to which the Ergon is hooked, which stretches*) *between the stage and the central door of the the-atre, the Ergon slides quickly, as if flying, over the heads of the audience.*)

THE RED MAN — The Tower of Raun is threatening. Volan - the creator and the builder - has not been able to accomplish his goal. Thus it should be partially demolished and immediately rebuilt. (*to Volan*) What do you think - comrade?

VOLAN — The tower will be razed to the ground - and to its foundations - the people of Raun will gather to recognize their liberation.

SACAR — Don't listen to him - my Lord! The power of Volan is beyond human. Seeing his creature stagger - his brain has been struck by lightening!

VOLAN — Why is the female Sacar trying to make excuses for me? Why is she calling me crazy? I am not crazy - I shall not stop - the creator goes ever forward - always anticipates. I will create a new humanity - one which is free from machines.

SACAR — This confirms his madness.

THE RED MAN — Why punish humanity with the anguish of the spirit? We have the greatest civilization: the electromechanical civilization. Each individual is a cog in this great machine - in this absolute perfection of life. We have found the source of true happiness. The egoism of races no longer exists - we are but a single race. Our few children do not carry in their blood the decadence of their parents. All is order - discipline. The machine - our divine and adored creature - has taught us perseverance - moderation - precision. We do not want anything else. For this civilization - for this perfection - for this harmony of life - we wanted to erect the greatest monument - to which we have sacrificed everything.

THE ERGONS — (*in loud voices*) Long live the tower! Long live Raun!

THE RED MAN — (*to Volan*) The electric prison welcomes you! Let the rays of Electricity - our Almighty Mother - destroy the germs of your humanitarian madness.

VOLAN — Your word is law.

SILLAN — (*to Volan*) I was against you - due to my excess of love for you!

VOLAN — I forgive you.

SILLAN — You will only be absent. Your spirit lives in mine - it will be here with me to thrust your metallic architecture to dizzying heights.

VOLAN — My comrade - one day you will also be with me! (*with head bowed he slowly walks away; he enters the elevator, followed by four Ergons. He disappears*).

THE RED MAN — Sillan is your boss!

VOICES — Always at the top - Sillan!

SACAR — Volan is the creator of the tower. Greet the creator! Glory to the creator!

EVERBODY — Viva Volan! Viva!

THE RED MAN — To work!

(*An airplane circles above the tower*)

SILLAN — For the Red Man - the brain engine of Raun - for Sacar - the joy of all the living - I swear that the tower will face the sun!

THE RED MAN — Sun - you who with your inexhaustible energy moves our machines and our hearts - fills us with your energy - let us live - Sun!

EVERYBODY — Let us live - Sun!

(*Electric bell*)

LOUDSPEAKER — The tower is collapsing! Save yourselves!

(*A rope ladder is thrown down from the airplane; the Red Man, Sacar and Sillan grab hold of it. The Ergons cram themselves into the elevators which rapidly descend. Squealing. Creaking. The scraping of metal. A tremendous crash. A thunderous uproar. Thudding. Booming. Screams. Cries.*)

II.

THE ELECTRIC PRISON

SCENE: *In the center, a red cubic construction, similar to a stage, with a staircase on each side. On top of it, another construction, rectangular; it is open in the front, silver-colored and is brightly illuminated. This is the electric prison where Volan is imprisoned.*
DOMINANT ATMOSPHERE: *violet.*

CHORUS — (*which cannot be seen*) Volan - who is keeping you imprisoned - who is torturing you - who is stabbing you - Volan!

VOLAN — Crystal needles - in waves - are piercing my flesh - now caressing me like the nerveless fingers of a tired lover - now ripping me apart like the claws of a tiger.

CHORUS — Why do you rebel? Where do you want to go?

VOLAN — Where do I want to go? Why do you ask me? I am going inside the corolla of a rose - I want to tear out the heart of this rose.

CHORUS — Where is the rose?

VOLAN — Don't look for it. The rose is red - if you look at it - it will become livid.

CHORUS — Let Electricity extirpate from your mind the bad plant.

Electricity

intoxication of the living

divine

daughter of the Sun.

Let Volan return to us!

VOLAN — People of Raun - the tower is here! - can you see it? - can you see me? - I'm at the top - I built it - kneel down! - worship me! Can't you see that Sacar is here - next to me? - now Sacar is mine - worship her! Where is the Red Man? The empire of Raun is now mine - and its female is mine. (*pause*) What is that down there? A whirling storm - is approaching ominously - a cloud of black arrows... a flock of eagles... they have seen Sacar. They are hurtling themselves on you... to devour you! But where is Sacar? Now they are coming at my eyes - my eyes - (*with a scream*) they have torn out my eyes...

CHORUS — Divine Electricity

save Volan!

VOLAN — The rose - under my eyelid... they have devoured the rose!

CHORUS — Over there Raun is burning.

Tall ovens are vomiting rivers of fire

that flow into the hearts of the Ergons

lovers of machines.

Machines beating metallic rhythms.
The hammers strike
The rods punch
The pulleys run.
Machines sing
the deeds of Raun.
Wake up - Volan
your sleep means death!

VOLAN — A freezing wind blows - I'm frozen stiff - Sacar's body is also frozen stiff - I don't feel it close to me anymore...

CHORUS — Cold is your heart.
The machine no longer sings for you.
The alcohol of life
is within the machine.

VOLAN — The eagles devour the silvery wires of light - darkness is pressing me into a funnel - my ferruginous blood drips.

CHORUS — The machines are drinking your blood
the machines are intoxicated by you
they dance around you
they are languid veiled ladies
abandoned by you.

(THE DANCE OF THE MACHINES. *The light that illuminates the prison is extinguished. Dancer-machines appear and mime around Volan. When the rhythmic movement ends, they disappear. The light in the prison goes on again.*)

VOLAN — What is this deafening din that is splitting my ears? How many trucks are packed into that back alley! Torches in the night sway - the

Temple of the Sun is rising. But who is getting off that litter? I know her... (*calling*) Calpurnia! Calpurnia!

SACAR — (*she comes in, looks at Volan, and sits on the front staircase*) You are in pain - Volan!

VOLAN — I called you - Calpurnia! Tell me: do I still have your chain at my feet?

SACAR — What is this chain?

VOLAN — My feelings.

SACAR — I'm not Calpurnia. I'm Sacar - the Great Prostitute.

VOLAN — You are Calpurnia - you are in my blood.

SACAR — The Red Man has subjected you to electric martyrdom. I can see a flame in your mind - the fog of the past is burning. You are turning into the great architect again.

(*The Architect enters the scene, like a ghost, robed in antiquated Roman attire.*)

VOLAN — My life is like a camellia - without scent - shut inside the mechanism of its own beauty.

ARCHITECT — I am the builder - I built the Temple of the Sun God.

SACAR — (*frightened*) Who are you?

ARCHITECT — Aterio. I lived.

SACAR — Aterio? You lived?

ARCHITECT — Can you not remember me?

SACAR — No.

ARCHITECT — Impossible. You never died - but I am dead - my spirit is here - I regained my body only so that I could be recognized...

VOLAN — Calpurnia - you get off your litter - with a light step you advance between the bustling of slaves - your beauty stiffens them into statues - and the stones for building the temple fall from their hands... Wretches! What fascination this female holds! Pick up the stones and stone her! (*pause*) I can see your feline creeping behind my back - a blade makes my blood gush forth... (*pause*) Why did you kill me?

SACAR — I want you - Volan!

ARCHITECT — You still do not recognize me?

SACAR — I can't see you - but you speak like Volan.

ARCHITECT — My name is Aterio!

SACAR — I don't remember you - why do you want to be called this?

ARCHITECT — And why is your name Calpurnia? Why did you kill me?

VOLAN — Why do you still keep me with you? Let me go! Why do you keep scratching at my wound with your nails? Why do you still wander with my body? Eternal is your wandering.

SACAR — I want you - Volan!

ARCHITECT — (*coming forward*) I have come to you - you will not escape me!

SACAR — (*terrified*) Now I can see you!

ARCHITECT — Do you still care for me?

SACAR — Flee - disappear - go back to your past!

ARCHITECT — I want to uproot you from the earth - your roots are deep - you are poisoning the earth...

SACAR — What I am now - I was and will be - nothing can be changed - thus I must be...

ARCHITECT — Forever you live - you project yourself into your becoming - I too lived - projecting myself into Volan. Now Volan is no longer me - he has diverted his destiny. You are the diverter - you are diverting all of humanity - the heredity of evil is perpetual in you - from birth to birth you take it up again. This is why I will kill you. And for good. So that you will never be born again! (*he approaches Sacar. The scene darkens.*)

SACAR — (*screaming*) Volan! He is going to kill me! Volan - for you I must live!

(*A change in lighting. The Architect disappears. Volan, freed from prison, approaches Sacar who is stretched out on the staircase.*)

VOLAN — Where?... Here?... Was I dreaming?

SACAR — (*getting up*) Volan!

VOLAN — You?...

SACAR — I will set you free...

VOLAN — Are you setting me free? (*looking around*) Ah...

SACAR — I can do everything.

VOLAN — (*walking away*) I will go back to my place.

SACAR — Where do you want to go back to? Come here. Raun is in our hands - if you wish...

VOLAN — I will not conspire...

SACAR — I set you free - I will pay by my death!

VOLAN — What good is that?

SACAR — Go - escape from Raun! - You can no longer live here - go far away - other continents are deserted - establish your new world over there. Here it is impossible - here we must live our own life - all of us want to live this beautiful terrible life. (*Pause*) I spoke to you before as a female lover - but now I am Sacar - the queen - the Red Man's mate. I order you: leave! I have thought of everything...

VOLAN — You are the queen - I will obey you - I must obey you.

SACAR — I'm still in a "deadlock" - in our lives all of us have such a moment - we no longer belong to ourselves - our reason abandons us more and more - we abandon ourselves to the absolute - are guided by a cosmic force - are a toy in the hands of a will... (*pause*) Perhaps it is the superior life! (*pause*) This great moment... in me... has created a love for you... in you... has created the tower...

VOLAN — Yes... the "deadlock"... the great moment... is not the tower...

SACAR — (*with bitter surprise*) Is not the tower?... Then?...

VOLAN — Rescue Raun... rescue you... rescue everyone... machines... machines... machines without souls...

III.

THE GYNAEMACHINE

SCENE: *On the left: Sacar's throne surrounded by ten cylindrical constructions of various sizes. Above these cylinders, which are always slightly gyrating in motion, sits the Chorus.*
In the Center: the Gynaemachine - the construction and the shape of which are left to the imagination of the scenographer - which visits and classifies those Virgins of Raun who have reached puberty. When it is at work we can see the movements of levers, hands, wheels, etc. On a panel are bright multicolored letters and numbers. Based on the decision of the manager of the Gynaemachine, Virgins are used either for procreation (Category M.), pleasure (Cat. P.), or for labor (Cat. L.).
To the right: a large loudspeaker.
DOMINANT ATMOSPHER: *orange.*

LEFT CHORUS — Today is the day of the Virgins of Raun - the Gynaemachine will decide their destinies.

RIGHT CHORUS — Joy to the daughters of the machines who see Sacar - the luminous Queen.

LEFT CHORUS — Thousands upon thousands of them will come out of the gynaeceums - each one will live the beauty of the life of a machine.

RIGHT CHORUS — For the power of the Red Man - for the power of Sacar.

LEFT CHORUS — Happiness to those chosen by the divine Gynaemachine - happiness to the elect who will give children to the kingdom of Raun.

RIGHT CHORUS — They are mothers - machine producers of Raun.

LEFT CHORUS — Their wombs will be torn - but their breasts will remain intact.

RIGHT CHORUS — Happiness to those chosen by the divine Gynaemachine - happiness to the elect who will donate their bodies for the pleasure of the Initiates of Raun.

LEFT CHORUS — Happiness to these young women born for love - each male is the first lover.

RIGHT CHORUS — Infertile ones with virgin wombs - your bodies will experience nothing but pleasures.

LEFT CHORUS — You are the favorites of Sacar - the Infertile One.

RIGHT CHORUS — Machines of voluptuousness - your embrace gives our men the frenzy of life.

LEFT CHORUS — Happiness to those chosen by the divine Gynaemachine - happiness to the elect who will not experience the spasms of the flesh.

RIGHT CHORUS — You are Ergons - work machines - to you Raun entrusts her power.

LEFT CHORUS — Only in you is there great
   happiness.
CHORUS — (*together*) Sacar - daughter of the Moon
   - Goddess of infertility - Queen of the females
   of Raun.
SACAR — (*appearing on the throne*).
   Moon - my mother
   bride of the Sun
   you gave me to the light
   and died
   the cruelty of the omnipotent father
   eternally tortures you
   dragging along
   your cadaver.
   Moon - protect the infertile women of Raun
   caressing with your pallor
   the dreams of mothers
   so that their daughters
   remain infertile.
   We live to enjoy Raun
   are all captivated by love
   and always - Moon - pray to you:
   give us strong and cruel and handsome men
   who have in their veins the sparks of your Groom
   and who burn our bodies like torches
   and give us eternal youth.
CHORUS - Give us strong and cruel and handsome men
   who have in their veins the sparks of your Groom
   and who burn our bodies like torches
   and give us eternal youth.

(*The cylinders of the Chorus stop. The Gynaema-chine is turned on. At its sides stand Ber and the MAN-NUMBER.*)

SACAR — How many category M. females have given birth?

MAN-NUMBER — 3525 - 814 males - 2711 females.

SACAR — How many will be put to rest?

MAN-NUMBER — 307.

SACAR — How many category P. females have completed their ten years of service?

MAN-NUMBER — 23000.

SACAR — How many are needed for category L.?

MAN-NUMBER — 120000.

SACAR — How many breeders have been declared unfit?

MAN-NUMBER — 3200.

SACAR — Very well. Ber - present your annual report.

BER — (*motionless and without gestures*) The painful phenomenon of disproportionate female births requires the immediate modification of the life regimen of the breeders. Once the necessary studies and investigations have been carried out - we might well find that the breeders have been abandoned to an overly sedentary life. Idleness - frivolity - a great preoccupation with clothing - the search for dainty foods - the egotistical conservation of their energy - the preference for skinny females who to our misfortune the divine and infallible Gynaemachine has assigned to category M. etc. etc. have without doubt influenced and emasculated the breeders - and perverted their genetic sense.

SACAR — It is quite grave! You must find a solution immediately!

BER — From now on the breeders will be trained in a special gymnasium in the most violent athletic exercises. For each group of 10 only a single female will be granted - who will have to be won through bloody fights. We believe this is the most suitable remedy. Animal nature gives us absolutely irrefutable evidence on the matter.

SACAR — So be it.

BER — This year the request for human material has been somewhat complicated due to the rapid changes in Raun life. Having implemented the new regimen of breeders - a need for 5300 females in category M. has arisen. As for category P. - profound changes must be implemented. We have observed a slackness in the Initiates unprecedented in the machine era. All this is due to the fact that - after work - they are even besieged by a considerable number of females. Since this year the total number we need to retrain in this category - as they have reached their tenth year of service - is 23000 - we suggest replacing them with only 7000. In view to the greater amount of work - which is not completely undesirable - we could reduce the years of service from 10 to 8.

SACAR — With this I do not agree. I believe we need to increase the numbers - as in the Initiates an increasing need for fresh material has been observed.

BER — That is an intolerable sign of decadence! In this case we cannot assume the great responsibility of our position and will be forced - unwillingly - to resign from the high office of First Administrator of Sexual Services.

SACAR — Being such an exceptional measure - we ask - before it is put into effect - the opinion of our Master and Leader - the omnipresent Red Man.

LOUDSPEAKER — Let the decision of our First Administrator be followed.

SACAR — The word of the Red Man is law!

BER — As far as category L. is concerned - we believe the number 120000 to be insufficient. The machines are using an enormous number of Ergons. The building of the tower is continuously depleting our resources. Therefore we suggest the insertion of all who are available.

SACAR — Approved. Open the gynaeceum also - and let the divine and infallible Gynaemachine pronounce its sacred answers! (*The cylinders of the Choir begin to move. The Virgins who need to be classified by the Gynaemachine come near. They wear simple mechanic's outfits with numbers on the breasts. The girls, stiff automatic beings who respond to the number called by the MAN-NUMBER, go inside the Gynaemachine. The lights on the panel flash. After a few moments, the girls come out, with the appearance of the life they are destined to; they cross the stage, bow to Sacar, and then disappear through the exit behind the throne.*)

MAN-NUMBER — 88754.

(On the electric panel: Cat: P - 55,3/4 - AG 1/8 - B.)

CHORUS — Favorite of Sacar - you shall always be first in your mission as the machine for voluptuousness.

MAN-NUMBER — 88755.

(On the electric panel: Cat: L. - 75,1/20 - EH 1/3 - C.)

CHORUS — You have the bliss of renouncing your sex - extinguished in you is any desire of the flesh - the Red Man is grateful to you - you who are a work machine.

MAN-NUMBER — 88756.

(On the electric panel: Cat: M. - 63,1/4 - SC 1/70 - A)

CHORUS — You are the female amongst all females - sacred is your body - you are the machine that gives life.

MAN-NUMBER — 88757.

(On the electric panel: Cat: P. - 58,1/12 - HSO 20/50 - B)

CHORUS — Happiness to you who will never witness the withering of your beauty - the incandescent lips of the tall ovens will give you the final kiss.

BER — Halt! The percentage of category P. females is too high. The year 328 of our era was influenced by the passing of the V. 72 comet. The appearance of this comet - let it be damned! - was ominous. Volan - the Great Initiate - went mad - and the tower has not yet been completed. We suggest that class 329 be visited.

SACAR — The V. 72 comet - which is eternally damned - and which the Sun - my father - cast into the abyss - disturbing the titanic deed of Volan - and subjecting our kingdom to terrible consequences...

LOUDSPEAKER — Sillan - the one who continues the work of Volan - is coming to you - Sacar!

SACAR — Wait a moment!

(*Everyone departs*)

SILLAN — (*entering*) - Mighty Sacar - I shall never see the tower completed!

SACAR — You...

SILLAN — I feel alone.

SACAR — You accused Volan.

SILLAN — It's true. I did it for you.

SACAR — For me?

SILLAN — Volan had given up...

SACAR — Volan was suffering.

SILLAN — He had turned into a man.

SACAR — Volan was illuminated. The illuminated is always man.

SILLAN — I no longer see the tower.

SACAR — It's Volan's curse.

SILLAN — Only you can free Raun from this curse.

SACAR — All of Raun supports the tower.

SILLAN — I need all of it - but that is not enough...

SACAR — Raun can do all.

SILLAN — In five years we will not have a single ergon left!

SACAR — Has not everyone already been replaced by machines?

SILLAN — And who will build - who will create the new machines?

SACAR — Raun abounds in inventors.

SILLAN — One cannot invent when one no longer has a soul!

SACAR — You disowned Volan.

SILLAN — Volan wanted to destroy the tower - destroy the kingdom of the machines - annihilate the splendor of our epoch. It was impossible!

SACAR — Volan didn't want this.

SILLAN — You want to defend Volan?

SACAR — Volan is no longer in our kingdom - he is far away - for us he is dead.

SILLAN — In five years we will no longer have skilled ergons - the tower will never be completed - our epoch will collapse - we cannot do it in time...

SACAR — For us the meaning of time is unknown. Raun knows only the will.

SILLAN — The Gynaemachine must no longer exist!

SACAR — Sacrilege! Are you rebelling against our laws?

SILLAN — I must rebel against the laws - rebel against everyone - I only see the tower.

SACAR — The Gynaemachine is the sacred selectrice of our race - do you want to bastardize our race?

SILLAN — Open the gynaeceum! Let all the females become mothers! They need to give us human material - we need millions of ergons!

SACAR — This is the end of Raun!

SILLAN — It is the life of the tower!

SACAR — If all of our females are allowed to regenerate - if they are given the freedom to choose their males - sentiment - the leprosy of previous epochs - will be born again. The children - little by little - will lose the mechanical sense of life - their hearts will no longer feel the geometric splendor of the world - man will rebel against the absolute power of the leaders - they will deny us the right to decide their lives. This is the end of Raun!

SILLAN — You cannot stop eternal becoming. Life depends on an inexorable will - which is not yours - nor the Red Man's. All that needs to happen has been prearranged - no one can oppose it.

SACAR — As long as the Red Man and I live - it must be like this - and it shall be!

SILLAN — Empires and populaces are buried beneath desert sands - choked by forests - submerged in the ocean. Faith and truth - in which man believed firmly - for which he fought - destroyed - exterminated - no longer have any meaning… (*pause*) A few more years - and you will see me alone on the tower.

SACAR — You see everything in so terrifying a manner?

SILLAN — Nothing is terrifying. Our existence swings between two poles of absurdity.

SACAR — Our life has been completely cast into the vortex of machines - devoured by velocity. We haven't even a second to think - thought is our enemy. We have mechanized ourselves because we need to forget…

SILLAN — This magical attraction we feel for machines is the most delightful torture - but we Initiates still have a crumb of a soul - and beware if we are forced to look into its depths.

SACAR — Volan looked into the depths of his soul. Truth is a bottomless ocean.

SILLAN — Must I subject Raun to the greatest struggle - to the greatest sacrifice? Is this what you want?

SACAR — Go back up there - and do not let your faith waver. I know what you crave... I will be yours...

SILLAN — Well then... let it all perish! (*he places his lips on Sacar's foot. Troubled he exits.*)

LOUDSPEAKER — Let the inspection resume immediately. Before sunrise - the 5,300 category M. females must be at work.

SACAR — We will rapidly proceed. Class 328 has given almost negative results. Let us move on...

LOUDSPEAKER — If class 329 is also unfavorable to category M. - Ber must proceed with the modification of the mechanism of the Gynaemachine. Functional capacity must drop from 100% to 80%. All this will unsettle our statutes - but it is also necessary. All the ergons have been mobilized by Sillan for the reconstruction of the tower.

SACAR — May the Gynaemachine be benevolent!
(*Once again the scene is filled with young ladies in various costumes. Ber, the Man-number, and the Choir, go back to their places.*)

MAN-NUMBER — 102515.
(*On the electric panel: Cat: P. - 53,2/3 - VG ¼ - B*)

CHORUS — Let your eyes envelop all in the flames of your desires.

MAN-NUMBER — 102516
(*On the electric panel: Cat. P. - 54,21/24 - MA 1/75 - B*)

CHORUS — Grind your lovers in the gears of your lust.

MAN-NUMBER — 102517
(*Suddenly the Gynaemachine stops working. The lights dim.*)

BER — Disaster! Disaster! The Gynaemachine has stopped working!
(*Astonishment, distress in the crowd.*)

SACAR — (*approaching the Gynaemachine*) - Divine Gynaemachine!

CHORUS — The young woman inspected is impure
the Gynaemachine has stopped
her wrath cannot be placated
unless the guilty one is executed.
(*The female exits the Gynaemachine. There is a murmuring in the crowd.*)

LOUDSPEAKER — Do not touch the female! The shame of Raun!

BER — Wretch! - who are you?

SAIB — I'm the female Saib - a useless machine in the kingdom of Raun.

BER — What crime have you committed?

SAIB — I haven't committed a crime.

LOUDSPEAKER — Confess to me alone!

SACAR — The all-seeing Red Man commands.
(*The scene darkens. Sacar exits followed by the chorus. All the others leave the scene shortly thereafter. Only Saib remains. Spotlights shine green light on the loudspeaker, gradually gaining in intensity, un-*

til the character's attributes can be seen. When the loudspeaker makes its voice heard, it rhythmically emits white light from its cone.)

LOUDSPEAKER — Do you know why the Gynaemachine - the infallible regulatrice of Raun - has refused to make you live our life?

SAIB — (*curtly*) No.

LOUDSPEAKER — Your crime is without equal - to take your life is hardly sufficient!

SAIB — I don't want that - I cannot die.

LOUDSPEAKER — I - the supreme judge of Raun - before deciding your fate - want to hear from you what you think of your crime. I rule out the possibility that individuals of the opposite sex might have penetrated into the gynaeceums. I rule out the possibility that the females might have maternal feelings towards their children. So I ask: why did you not kill your son? You could have at least tried to conceal your guilt.

SAIB — If - lofty mind of Raun - all this is inexplicable to you - it is for me as well. I am pure.

LOUDSPEAKER — I see all - now confess!

SAIB — On certain nights - while asleep - it seemed to me that I was being transported somewhere. I would wake up in the arms of a man who spoke to me in an incomprehensible language… I remember that this man was no longer young - his voice was sharp - sometimes thick - sometimes tender. Later… I began to understand this strange language… but I must have dreamed it all because I haven't seen that man since…

(*pause*). How could my child be a stranger to me?... How could I have killed him?...

LOUDSPEAKER — Your crime is to have "humanized" yourself. Here everything is mechanized - nothing human is allowed to exist in our kingdom. The germs of this damned humanity have however not been completely destroyed... I - the supreme judge - inexorable but just - cannot condemn you. But everything that has happened can have fatal consequences on Raun. I order you to immediately leave our kingdom. An airplane will take you to another land...

SAIB — (*trembling*) With my son... right?

LOUDSPEAKER — As for your son - for the salvation of Raun - that seed must be diffused. Here - or elsewhere - your son - having been conceived by "humanized" beings - would become the greatest danger to machine civilization. I condemn your son to death!

SAIB — (*desperately*) No! No! Spare my son! Kill me instead! Have pity on my son!

LOUDSPEAKER — Your son is no longer alive!

SAIB — (*she faints*)

IV.

AIRPLANE 85317

SCENE: *an island. Forest. Hut. Volan has returned to the state of primitive man.*
DOMINANT ATMOSPHERE: *between green and turquoise.*

VOLAN — (*hollowing out a tree trunk*) Escape from here… from this solitude… at the mercy of the ocean… leave it to chance… disappear… What does it matter? The forest is strangling me with quiet vines - the singing of the birds is more ferocious than the whirling of machines… The electric prison was for me more soothing! (*pause*) Night is falling: the moon - a plump surgeon - smiling in its gown of pearls - nails me to the forest's green table - carves out my heart - and smiles - always smiles… (*pause*) The sun rises: the trees become very tall and slim smokestacks… the streams run with hot steel…

(*pause*) What is the location of this accursed island? Is it at the antipodes of Raun? Never a ship - never an airplane to be seen! When did I get here? I've lost all notion of time. (*he touches his body*) But I don't feel old yet... I need to begin to live again... in this canoe I shall grapple with the sea... trying to keep its green jaws from swallowing me...

(*The light fades away. Distant, at first unclear, then increasingly distinct, the sound of an airplane engine. Volan cannot help but make a gesture of wonder. He raises his eyes towards the sky. Now the roar of the engine is becoming louder. The powerful eye of a searchlight scours the forest, then stops and steadily fixes itself on Volan.*)

VOLAN — (*dazzled, he lifts his hands to his eyes. He is gripped by a strong emotion*) Now... now... I am beginning to live... live... live (*with joy he raises his hands into the air. A deep and mighty rumbling*) It's here already... veering... veering... down... gliding... bringing me life... I feel it... (*suddenly a blaze of light flashes through the sky. Volan lets out a piercing cry*) it has brought death... (*he runs towards the beach*)

(*Change of lighting. Volan and Saib carry the Captain in their arms, whose face is blackened and clothes burnt. They lay him on the ground.*)

SAIB — Something to help relieve his pain - bandages - he has serious burns.

VOLAN — I don't have anything - only water - water is the only medicine here...

SAIB — The airplane is submerged near the shore - at present nothing can be recovered… we must treat his wounds somehow… (*they undress him.*)

VOLAN — (*to the Captain, shaking him gently*) How do you feel? Where are you from? Who are you?

CAPTAIN — (*making an effort he points to his chest*) Here…

VOLAN — K. S. 8258.

SAIB — A number!

CAPTAIN — (*gasping*) Let me die… my body is a burning torch… throw me into the sea… this female cannot… must not stay here… by order of the Red Man… in my pocket there should be a pistol… look… I can't…

SAIB — (*terrified, she looks at Volan*) Yes - yes - quick - it's better that I die - but far away - far away from the furnaces of Raun. (*pause*) - Are you hesitant? If you don't wish to be the Red Man's executioner - then let your men kill me…

VOLAN — Here I am king and… the sole subject.

SAIB — You are alone? But why? Where are we?

VOLAN — I don't know. A secluded island - an airplane brought me here as well - much time has passed - I haven't counted the days - the years…

SAIB — You too… are from Raun?

VOLAN — (*hesitant*) Yes… (*pause*) Can you calculate… well… more or less… the amount of time that passed… from when you left - to the time of the crash? The speed of the airplane? We could approximately establish if we are still on earth or on another planet! I have always had the impression of being on another planet!

SAIB — I couldn't tell... it didn't seem as if we were flying over either land or sea - we shot into the ocean of space - like a thunderbolt. Speed captivated me - intoxicated me like a strong narcotic...

VOLAN — Well then we are quite far away...

CAPTAIN — What is this female talking about? She shouldn't know anything. I tell you once more: execute the order... it is my directive...

VOLAN — I only know how to command.

CAPTAIN — (*moving his body in an attempt to get up and throw himself upon the female*) The Re Re Rrrrred Maaaaaaaaannnn (*falling heavily*)

SAIB — The executioner of Raun.

VOLAN — His last moments.

CAPTAIN — (*in agony*) Kill that female... she is going to bring you bad luck... try to save the plane's papers... you will know everything... you... you... you...

VOLAN — He's gone.

SAIB — Fulfill his final wish. Let the sea accept his tormented body!

VOLAN — There is a very high cliff here that juts out over the - and beneath the sea is an abyss. One who loved the sky - who loved heights - cannot rest beneath the earth - so let him repose in the abyss.

SAIB — You speak like some hallucinated from Raun!

VOLAN — I am from Raun - I glorified Raun - and want to return to Raun!

SAIB — (*frightened*) Why didn't I perish in the catastrophe? Why did you not want to kill me?

VOLAN — Raun must have changed. Can a female of the Red Man's Metropolis talk this way?

SAIB — I was born in Raun. There was a turning point in my life - and I felt like a stranger. This is why I was ostracized.

(*Walking like automata, two air mechanics from the airplane, who were able to save themselves, appear on the scene. On their chests the registration numbers: Tr. P. 12345 and Tr. P. 67890. They stop at a distance. Volan motions for them to come closer*).

VOLAN — You had a narrow escape!

AIR MECHANIC I. — We saved ourselves with parachutes.

SAIB — It's a miracle that I am alive. They shut me inside a cabin when we departed. When the airplane began to burn... I didn't see any hope of escape... I don't know how... I found myself safe and sound on the waves...

VOLAN — (*to the air mechanics*) How many people were in the crew?

AIR MECHANIC II. — Nine.

VOLAN — And the others?

AIR MECHANIC I. — Sunk with the airplane.

VOLAN — This man?

AIR MECHANIC II. — The Captain.

VOLAN — He died just now. (*pause*) There is a promontory over there. Tie an engine to his ankles. Dead - he can still be on his feet! Throw him into the ocean! (*to the dead man*) Goodbye! You obeyed the laws of Raun - I bid you farewell -

old comrade! (*to the air mechanics*) Go! (*the two take the cadaver away*) Now we need to recover what is left of the airplane… its papers…

SAIB — The Captain is slowly descending into the abyss. I would have thought that with him even my memory of Raun would disappear for good. And yet two ghosts rise up from the wreckage. It's the Red Man who is persecuting me.

VOLAN — With four of us - it will be easier to leave this beguiling and malicious island.

SAIB — Fate wanted me to be with you - far away - away from the Devouring Metropolis - able to live a new life - and you…

VOLAN — I cannot stay here. See that tree trunk… I had already made up my mind…

SAIB — Now that I'm in an unfamiliar world - on this blessed island - where the sea - the birds - the trees - the springs - the streams fill my soul with new melodies - where I have met the exiled… (*pause*) And since you have been exiled - you must possess something that nobody else in Raun has - something which Raun fights against… (*pause*) Flee from this quiet - this unique peace - and immolate yourself in the fires of Raun… But… are you a man or a machine?

VOLAN — I am a man!

SAIB — Then do you wish to become a machine?

VOLAN — I want to save "these machines".

SAIB — Now I understand why you are here. (*The two air mechanics return*).

AIR MECHANIC I. — Everything has been done!

VOLAN — Try to find - among the wreckage - the plane's papers.

AIR MECHANIC II. — I have here with me some papers which might be useful. (*from his jacket he takes out a sheaf of papers*). A wave pushed them onto the beach. (*He hands them to him*)

VOLAN — The flight log. (*leafing through the pages*) "Airplane 85317 - Flight 873 - Captain etc. - Crew etc." - (*to the air mechanics*) Go! Try to salvage as much as you can from the airplane. Anything might be useful to us! (*The two leave*). The last annotations: "11.20 a.m. of the 14th - 11th month - year 345 of the Era of Machines - Radio: 128: By order of the Red Man - the female Saib is to be transported to island N.W. 1185 and left there. From Raun the airplane will head directly to island W. N. W. 421. Check with maximum attention whether the ex-Initiate Volan still shows signs of life. On the return flight etc. etc."

SAIB — Volan! The man of the Tower!

VOLAN — The man who did not want the tower. But - it isn't important who I was. (*he continues leafing through the pages*) We have the exact distance: 3800 miles from Raun. How can we cover it without flying machines? The diary of the Captain is also here. The last lines: "10 a.m. of the 14th - 11th month: I am embarking on a trip of no return. I am transporting the female Saib to her exile. I take misfortune with me.

Why did the Supreme Judge of the Metropolis not put the wretched one who violated the law to death? Why was this accursed woman allowed to give birth to a child before the Gynaemachine was able to decide on its destiny? Misfortune for Raun! Misfortune for me! That this vile female is damned!"

SAIB — I'm damned because I have a soul…

VOLAN — And our son?

SAIB — (*throwing her arms around Volan. A long pause, during which both need to express the intense emotion at finding each other again*). Killed… all that is yours is lost… but now… I've found you again!

VOLAN — When I became "human" again I knew what to expect: the electric prison. With un-paralleled courage I risked entering into the gynaeceums. I met you… joined you… I hoped that one day a being would be born able to take revenge for me…

SAIB — I hear your voice again! It's a dream!

VOLAN — Raun awaits us.

SAIB — There is nothing any longer that keeps us attached to Raun.

VOLAN — As long as Raun exists - our place is there.

SAIB — In the concrete and iron labyrinths of the Metropolis - humanity has forgotten the sources of life. The child of the earth attacks its mother.

VOLAN — Raun knows that the earth is dying - its womb has been condemned to be barren. Machines - which can do everything - are unable to stop the great law!

SAIB — The air is becoming thinner - the water is drying up. The earth will become a world of death - rolling black and useless through space. No machine can conquer death!

(*The air mechanics re-enter the scene. They carry with them several instruments and a small radio device*).

AIR MECHANIC I. — The low tide has returned the airplane to us - it's completely unserviceable. We salvaged the plane's instruments. The radio device is intact.

VOLAN (*joyfully*) — Death for us will be beaten by this machine! (*he takes the device and sets it up so that it will work*).

SAIB — What are you doing?

VOLAN — I'll contact an airplane to take us to Raun.

SAIB — (*with resignation*) Your will be done!

VOLAN — (*to the air mechanics*) We need your flight suits. Go into the hut and change them. (*The two obey. Volan operates the radio*) Hello! Hello Raun! Airplane 85317 has caught fire… has fallen into the ocean near island W. N. W. 421… crew completely lost… aside from two air mechanics. We were able to save the radio and plane's papers. Our numbers: Tr. P. 12345 and Tr. P. 67890.

LOUDSPEAKER - Island W. N. W. should be inhabited. Tell us who you have seen.

VOLAN — The only thing is a hut that has clearly not been occupied for a long time ago.

(*The air mechanics bring the flight suits*).

LOUDSPEAKER — We will send out a rescue plane immediately.

VOLAN — (*to the air mechanics*) We will be leaving soon. An airplane is coming to get us. You will stay here. Hide yourselves in the deepest part of the forest. No one should be aware of you. Maybe one day you will see me again…

AIR MECHANIC I. — Our life is in the air!

AIR MECHANIC II. — Without flight - death…

AIR MECHANICS — (*together*) Long live Raun! Viva! (*they depart*).

(*Volan and Saib put on the flight suits*).

SAIB — In every epoch love has created.

VOLAN — And love has destroyed.

SAIB — The end of an era.

VOLAN — The beginning of another.

SAIB — A civilization destroyed.

VOLAN — Another will be created.

SAIB — From nebulas stars are born.

VOLAN — And from stars nebulas.

SAIB — Resurrection of space!

VOLAN — Time is All!

(*The sound of a fast-approaching airplane*).

SAIB — Love is life.

(*With mechanical gestures they start to walk slowly towards the beach*).

SAIB — Here comes the airplane!

VOLAN — Kill your emotions - we are now automatons!

V.

THE TRANSPLANETARY DOCKYARD

SCENE: *a corner of the transplanetary dockyard. Fervor of activity. Orderly bustling around of the ergons. Music-noises of the enormous workshop. Loudspeaker.*
DOMINANT ATMOSPHERE: *red.*

ERGONS: — (*walking around the stage, carrying in their hands or on their shoulders, either alone or in groups, detached parts of the sideroship made of various types of metal; pieces taken from electric engines; large oxygen tanks; work tools, etc. etc. The following words need to be orchestrated to the sound of the workshop*) Gears - pulleys - rods - pistons - valves - propellers - wheels - flywheels - turbines - dynamos - magnets - presses - hammers - lubricants - quick - quick - quick - shell part 117 - here is 1118 - assembly 211 on the left - test - test - pass - quick…
LOUDSPEAKER — Faster!

ERGONS — (*accelerating their movements*) Fireballs - projectiles - armored - rocket - tank - mixture - liquid oxygen - alcohol - ignition - combustion - explosion chamber - detonator - fire - fire - fire - gold - yellow - yellow - infernal - propulsion - launch - Raun - hiss - hiss - climb - dizziness - lightning - Mars - air - air - pressure - heaviness - drowsiness - asphyxiation - cold - frost - 273 degrees - attrition - out - out...

LOUDSPEAKER — Run!

ERGONS — (*running*) We - we - we ergons - men of steel - racing machines - machines - machines - racing - tireless - beautiful machines - conquer - conquer - conquer death - we - we - we ergons - life of Raun - tower builders - capture - capture - capture stars - universes - conquer - conquer - conquer death…

LOUDSPEAKER — Stop!

ERGONS — (*they freeze, each in their own posture*).

SILLAN — (*appearing*) Ergons - your seed shall flourish on Mars! There you will take our mechanical civilization!

ERGONS — Mars! Mars! Ours! Ours!

SILLAN — I built the tower that rules over all of earth's mountains - I built the first sideroship. Our brothers are already on planet Mars. They have sent us the message. They await us.

ERGONS — We are ready! Ready! Ready!

SILLAN — And now the second interplanetary flight. The Red Man and Sacar will take possession of Mars.

ERGONS — Viva Raun! Viva the Red Man! Viva Sacar! Viva Sillan!

SILLAN — Some of you - who built the M. 2 - shall receive the coveted reward of accompanying the Red Man.

ERGONS — (*pushing forward and raising their hands*) Me! Me!

SILLAN — Everybody to their places! The Red Man and Sacar will be here soon. The sideroship will be launched into space. (*The ergons leave with Sillan. Volan and Saib enter onto the scene. They are wearing the flight suits from scene 4*).

VOLAN — The time draws near…

SAIB — You will see Sacar again…

VOLAN — I want to… she must still be beautiful!

SAIB — I have pity for her… for everybody…

VOLAN —Sillan triumphs.

SAIB — Their end will be frightening.

VOLAN — It will be the most beautiful death. No human being has yet experienced this kind of death. To precipitate into sidereal space… eternally… And then? Maybe they will be swallowed up by a sun…

SAIB — They are going to have to suffer a great deal!

VOLAN — The speed will kill them instantly.

SAIB — It's horrible!

VOLAN — It's this life that is horrible! Never death!

LOUDSPEAKER — Ergons - run to meet the Red Man! Run to meet Sacar! They are the masters of the cosmos!

(*A crowd of ergons, with Sillan in the lead, pours onto the left half of the stage, arranging themselves in a semi-circle. From the right-hand side, the Red Man and Sacar majestically enter, followed by a group of Initiates. Volan and Saib are hidden among the ergons, although remaining in the foreground*).

SILLAN — Almighty Despot! Radiant Sacar! Today the civilization of Machines is offering you the greatest of all conquests: planet Mars. A bold handful of our comrades is already there. You shall now hear their voices. (*He operates a small device which has just then been brought to him*) Hello! Hello! Mars! How are you?

LOUDSPEAKER — Hello Raun! Hello! We are excellent… we are in a world that once was… we have undertaken the exploration of several areas… everywhere the vestiges of a superior civilization… living beings can probably no longer be encountered… but from what we have here… before our astonished eyes… it is impossible not to believe that Martians went to Earth millions of years ago… And after much delay we are returning the visit! (*Pause*). Meanwhile send us females… they are needed…

THE RED MAN — We will provide you with everything - it's appropriate!

SACAR — (*to Sillan*) Have fifty young women - the most beautiful - put on board the sidership!

SILLAN — Impossible. There isn't enough room. All seats have been taken until the sixth trip.

THE RED MAN — (*speaking into the device*) Pioneers of Mars - I offer you my greetings. You are honorable sons of the goddess Machine - who vanquishes all. What is left for you to do on this decrepit Earth? Nothing whatsoever! We have made the very last idols kneel at our feet. We have overcome the fear of God and the idea of Destiny. God is man - man is God! Initiates and ergons of Raun! The creative faculties of our civilization are nearly exhausted. But your courage remains - your heroism remains - which you have lifted up to the stars! Pioneers of Mars - navigators of Space! Your inventive genius will take you to other planets yet - and to others always! You have dissolved immeasurable distances. You have pushed Death away! Initiates and ergons of Raun - Pioneers of Mars! Man is God!

SILLAN — The sideroship is ready. Let us depart. Many of these ergons - Sacar - are worthy of flying with us. But there is only room for but a very few. Choose the fortunate and award them - with your smile comfort those who will stay behind.

SACAR — (*inspecting the ergons, she chooses three, who step forward. Then her eyes rest on Volan. She stares at him, seeming to recognize him, and turns pale, unable to stop a scream. More ergons. She is dazed.*) Come - here there are still the senses - life is over there - you must live there!

THE RED MAN — Man is God!

SILLAN — Glory to Raun!

(*The Red Man, Sacar and Sillan, followed by the Initiates, exit*).

ERGONS — (*in loud voices*) Raun! Raun! Raun!

Red Man! Red Man! Red Man!

Sacar! Sacar! Sacar!

Sillan! Sillan! Sillan!

(*The stage slowly empties. Volan and Saib are still there. Suddenly, sirens wail. Then a loud roar followed by a piercing hiss. The earth shakes. The sideroship has taken off. Cries of enthusiasm: Raun! Raun! Raun!*).

LOUDSPEAKER — Hello! Hello! Raun! Hello! We have detected the signs of departure - we will expect you in eleven hours. We will signal - for your arrival - our exact location.

VOLAN — They have gone. Raun has been liberated! (*he embraces Saib*).

LOUDSPEAKER — Sideroship departed with an initial extreme velocity. 7222 meters per second. It is hopeful that nothing grave has occurred on board.

SAIB — Volan - do you have a thirst for power?

VOLAN — Little female - it was not I who wanted it. I shall go back to being a lowly fellow… a wretched one…

SAIB — And if all fails? What if the speed device - which you altered - were to correct itself - and the sideroship reaches Mars!

VOLAN — I am Volan - I still consider myself a master of machines!

LOUDSPEAKER — At the present moment terrestrial attraction is being overcome. In two minutes the sideroship will reach the neutral zone.

SACAR — (*running onto the stage, breathless, she throws herself on Volan and shakes him. Saib stands motionless*) Volan! It's you! You're here? You're not dead? But is it really you? Let me take a look at you! Yes! It's you! But how? How is it that you are here at the dockyard? Speak! Speak!

VOLAN — I am Volan. Impossible to be recognized. But the female Sacar did.

SACAR — (*throwing her arms around his neck*) Let me look at you! Let me look at you!

VOLAN — Why didn't you leave? Why?

SACAR — I don't know. I don't know. Don't ask. I was next to the Red Man - next to him - trembling with joy for this trip into the marvels of the infinite. Sillan was giving the final orders. All of a sudden my mind became cloudy... I couldn't see anything... couldn't hear anyone... I rushed down the stairs of the gangway... found myself on the embankment... and at that moment the sideroship shot upward... and disappeared...

VOLAN — And now?

SACAR — Now the Tower of Raun's antennas will send the jubilation for your return into space. Now you are ours! (*holding him tightly*) Now you are mine - Volan!

LOUDSPEAKER — The sideroship is entering the orbit of Mars. The velocity - instead of decreasing -

continuously increases. We fear that the controls are not working properly.

VOLAN — Since the moment I no longer wanted to rebuild the tower - I have not been Volan. I only carry the name. Does my name trouble you?

SACAR — It isn't your name. It's your genius that troubles me. It's your body that troubles me. I am yours.

VOLAN — What can I give you? My compassion?

SACAR — (*exasperated*) Why am I here? Who called me here?

VOLAN — You who still has a soul - will suffer for all those whose souls you have torn away! You will suffer for everyone! It's your punishment!

SACAR — You can be free of me: kill me! Otherwise I'll always be your shadow!

LOUDSPEAKER — The sideroship is traveling at 1100 Km. a second. Due to its staggering speed Mars has been unable to draw it in. It is now once more outside orbit. It is drifting aimlessly in space. All is lost!

SACAR — Damn you! Damn you - Volan! You have killed the Despot - you have killed Sillan - you have annihilated Raun!

VOLAN — What needed to happen - has happened! You alone - Sacar - have been able to trick death! You are not my shadow - you are the shadow of Raun!

SACAR — So it was said: I had to follow the Victor - but I will not be your slave! (*she flees*).

SAIB — Vengeance is female - now we are in her hands - I'm happy to die with you!

VOLAN — We too can die! The reign of Machines is over!

(From the wings a slow rhythmic funereal step is heard. A crowd of ergons, hammers on their shoulders, heads bowed, advance onto the stage).

SAIB — Here they are! (*embracing Volan*) May our sacrifice be fruitful!

LOUDSPEAKER — Initiates of Raun! Ergons! Sacar is talking to you from the top of the tower. The Red Man and Sillan are navigating in celestial space. They will never return among you. They are united with the Whole! (*Pause*) Your queen - Sacar - your only dream of beauty and of flesh - will follow them. (*Pause*) Volan - alive again - Volan - the sublime spirit of Raun - is your leader. Adore him as I have adored him! Love him as I have loved him! (*Pause*) All men of Raun - these are the last words of your queen. (*All the workshops respond with the shrill sounds of sirens. Then suddenly all is silent*).

LOUDSPEAKER — Sacar has thrown herself off the tower!

VI.

THE DEATH OF THE MACHINES

SCENE: *a beach. Tropical forest. Three men, wearing primitive clothing, sit on the sand. Their gazes scan the sky.*
DOMINANT ATMOSPHERE: *azure.*

MAN I. — Nothing?

MAN II. — Nothing! (*Pause*).

MAN I. — This delay is inconceivable...

MAN II. — They were supposed to arrive this morning...

MAN I. — It's already evening!

MAN III. — Without radio...

MAN II. — Everyone is anxious.

MAN I. — There is nothing to be worried about. Volan is in charge of this final transport.

MAN III — A rebellion might have broken out!

MAN II. — Oh please! A rebellion! All the people wanted to leave Raun - of their own free will...

MAN I. — Only the word of Volan is true.

MAN II. — Liberation… rebirth…

MAN III. — And yet a rebellion must have broken out!

MAN I. — Who would not obey Volan?

MAN III — But I'm telling you: since the final transport still hasn't arrived - a rebellion is certain. The machines have rebelled!

MAN II. — The machines?

MAN III. — Exactly - the machines!

MAN I. — What madness! Volan has them tight in his grip!

MAN III. — Before. But now no longer!

MAN II. — Nonsense!

MAN III. — What was your work in Raun?

MAN II. — I worked as a chemist. I was in charge of artificial food.

MAN III. — I instead had the privilege to test engines. (*with regret*) No longer can I listen to their harmonious songs!

MAN II. — Infernal songs - songs of death!

MAN III. — But you also had to give up practicing chemistry! All for the benefit of our stomachs and our health! Here - just a few steps away - the forest has laid out a table for us that is of the greatest variety - and always sumptuous!

MAN I. — You too miss the machines! But you forget that during our voyage - the airplane you were piloting - almost slaughtered all of us…

MAN III. — Obviously! The engines were grieving - were sobbing. I tried to comfort them - but they showed themselves to be unwilling. Many times they disobeyed me. I lived through dreadful moments. (*Pause*) One of the engines was so furious - defiantly roaring all its contempt at me and urging the others to stop working. I commanded an air mechanic to recall it to order energetically. It was useless. I had to brutally punish it. I denied it oil - and soon after cut off the water. To make it die slowly - cruelly - taking pleasure in its sufferings. I was heartless - I know. But it was necessary to give proof of my authority - to give an example to the other engines. But things became worse than ever. In solidarity all the engines stopped...

MAN I. — ... and I still don't know how we are alive!

MAN III. — It's natural! The machines knew that they were no longer loved. They screamed at the betrayal - they wanted to take revenge...

MAN II. — Our great love for machines brought us to slavery - a double slavery: slaves of the machines - slaves of the ferocious Initiates of Raun.

MAN III. — Isn't the machine a creature of our own brain? - isn't it an extension of our own body? - doesn't its heart beat in the same way as ours?

MAN I. — We too should have become machines!

MAN III. — But we never would have been able to achieve the same level of perseverance - sincerity - miraculous precision...

SAIB — (*coming out from the forest, she approaches*).

MAN II. — Here comes Saib! Quiet.

MAN III. — No being in the world has been more faithful than the machine!

SAIB — As long as we remain on this earth - no one will ever be happy!

MAN I. — The machines had to bring us to another world. Leave us here forever. Maybe we will never talk like this again.

MAN III. — We have become men again - but our lives are and will always be artificial. Our souls have fled us - our brains have driven them away…

MAN II. — If our inner life doesn't exist - why do we still want to live?

SAIB — Volan - why are you not here - to respond to these unhappy men? You - who sacrificed everything for them.

MAN III. — (*ironically*) But you are here - Saib!

SAIB — The female can give you nothing but love - and sometimes comfort. Only Volan can illuminate your spirit!

(*Roaring of engines, at first barely perceptible, then increasingly more distinct*).

MAN I. — (*raising a hand to his ear*) The roar of engines!

MAN II. — The air fleet is coming!

EVERYBODY — (*looking up, they advance towards the shore*) Yes! Yes! They're coming!

SAIB — There in the lead is Volan's airplane - guiding the fleet!

MAN III. — The divine music of engines! I feel born again!

MAN II. — They are going to the bay!

MAN I. — They are landing over there!

SAIB — Let us go and greet Volan! Let us welcome our brothers! Now we are all united!

MAN III. — United! Very good! But detached from machines! Volan will be the first to need them. We will start over!

(*The scene remains deserted. The roaring intensifies to such an extent that it gives the impression that a fleet, made up of thousands of aircraft, has entered the theatre. Thus, including the stage, a proportionate number of rumble-makers will be positioned in the room and nearby. A shout of joy from the stage and the corridors*).

GIRL — (*holding the young man by the hand*) Come - come! We are alone - everyone is over there!

YOUNG MAN — Where are we going? I want to see the arrival of the air fleet! I want to see Volan!

GIRL — There will be enough time. Let's sit here for now - under the trees (*they sit down*).

YOUNG MAN — Why do you want us to stay alone? You're making me miss what I want to see. Do you need to talk to me? Why don't we talk over there - where everyone else is. I could see Volan.

GIRL — With all that confusion? To be bumped into and pushed and crushed by that screaming human flood. Here everything is so peaceful!

YOUNG MAN — I don't care. I want to see Volan!

GIRL — Don't you see me? Don't you like looking at me?

YOUNG MAN — (*in amazement*) We've seen each other many times! Didn't we make the voyage together? You were always near me… We looked at each other so many times…

GIRL — (*holding his hand*) You remember? You remember?

YOUNG MAN — Of course! The crossing was wonderful! I would have been happy if it had never ended! I was so delighted!

GIRL — And now who knows - if you will ever fly again!

YOUNG MAN — What? What? In Raun I was already a student pilot.

GIRL — But… we left Raun.

YOUNG MAN — I don't understand why. What is there to do here? A deserted beach - a forest full of spiteful monkeys - of vicious animals… Where are the wonderful workshops! At night it's totally dark. Everyone sleeps. Why then do they burn those big fires so far away? Raun - pulsating and feverish marvel of life - Raun - metropolis which never sleeps - Raun - irradiated by electrical moons!

GIRL — I prefer to be here - I'm happy - and even happier because I'm here alone with you. (*she pulls him to her*).

YOUNG MAN — (*hesitantly*) And so?…

GIRL — (*brushing against him with her face*) I wanted you here - alone - do you understand? I like you. I feel the need to be close to you - closer - (*she takes his head in her hands and kisses his hair and then his eyes*) No… I don't want to kiss your eyes… your eyes are cold… why are you looking at me like that?... Your grey eyes frighten me… it's your lips - that I want to kiss… your lips are bloodless! Where is your vitality? Where is your manhood? I will arouse you… I want to arouse life in you! (*she bites him savagely*).

YOUNG MAN — (*twisting free, with a cry*) You bit me! You bit me so I'm bleeding! Why? Why? (*he grabs her by her hair and shakes her with rage*) You're a beast!

GIRL — Yes - I'm a beast! Let me drink your blood! I want to drink your blood! (*she kisses him with vehemence*).

YOUNG MAN — (*with eyes closed, reeling*) Your scorching breath gives me life… I'm trembling all over… my vision is blurred… Can you feel how my heart is beating?… it feels as if it is about to burst… Swarms of wasps attack sting devour my irritated flesh… Now I can no longer see. It is the night that scatters handfuls of fireflies!

GIRL — Something is awakening in you!

YOUNG MAN — Yes! I feel it! I can feel it!

GIRL — (*she bares her chest and offers him her breasts*) Hold them - kiss - take - bite them - drink from them - quench your thirst… Now yes! You are a man! You are male! I want - want - want to be a mother! (*holding each other, they run into the forest*).

(*Change of lighting. Little by little the stage fills*).

MAN I. — Raun is dead - everything has stopped. Not a living soul was left there - the exodus has been completed.

MAN II. — All the matter - which we were condemned to knead and shape for the Red Man's rule - for the power of Raun - is now inert.

MAN III. — All the machines - all the airplanes are heaped up on the beach… dying…

MAN IV. — Save the machines! Without them we would never have been able to come here!

MAN V. — Let them be left as giants - as a testament to our madness!

MAN VI. — Free us from all temptation! Destroy them!

MAN VII. — Save the machines! Without machines - we shall perish!

MAN VIII. — (*pushing the others aside*) Make way! Make way! Here comes Volan!

EVERYONE — Volan! Volan! May your protection be upon us!

VOLAN — (*he enters, followed by two men; one is holding an energy condenser and a megaphone, the other is unwinding an electrical wire*) Is everything ready? (*in a broken voice*). To liberate ourselves from the machines - we must destroy the machines!

EVERYONE — (*screaming loudly*) Death to the machines!

MAN IX. — (*speaking through the megaphone*) Men - on your knees! This is your liberation!

EVERYONE — (*they kneel*)

(*Tragic silence. Volan, with decision, pushes the button. A tremendous explosion. The rush of air makes men and things sway. The sky turns red. Of all that was once machines nothing remains now but the name.*)

VOLAN — You are no longer machines - you are no longer slaves! Kiss the Earth! She is our Great Mother! (*everyone kisses the earth*) Work - suffer - love - hate - sometimes rejoice - often… not understanding each other... we are men!

THE END

(S. Lucia di Mela, May 1926 – Paris, September 1927)

RAUN

PLOT FOR CINEMATOGRAPHY

PART I.

Raun is the fantastic Metropolis of the Future. The Machine reigns supreme. Man, devoid of soul and sentiments, is an automaton at the mercy of the *Great Initiates* who are completely intent in a titanic endeavor of self-improvement in order to attain higher forms of life.

The Red Man, venerated like God, reigns despotically over the empire of Raun. He is the machine-brain: omnipotent, omnipresent, omniscient. By his side is *Sacar*, the beautiful cruel unrelenting queen sovereign, totally absorbed in her insatiable thirst of power.

In the center of the Metropolis, the *Ergons* work without respite, building the Tower of Raun, a metal structure which has to reach a height of ten thousands meters. This superhuman endeavor, destined to challenge time, space and God, shall remind posterity of the triumph of the electromechanical civilization.

Volan is the architect of this magnificent project and in its execution is assisted by his faithful disciple *Sillan*, who is completely spellbound by his teacher's work.

The tower rises up: beacons placed at intervals indicate its height. Nine thousands meters have already been reached. The inviolate peak of Everest has been overtaken by the genius of man.

And it is now that a strange phenomenon occurs. The tower sways. Warning sirens wail mournfully. The seismometers indicate a level four magnitude.

In the Office of Work Supervision, Volan and Sillan look at each other in astonishment. A few moments of fear go by, endless for those who experience them. On the last scaffold where the ergons are at work, a luminous panel shows the warning: *Stop!* Everything stops in a tragic silence. What has happened?

At the 7000-meter mark the pylons are bent. The dorsal spine of the cyclopean structure is giving in. The mountain of iron and steel will collapse, destroying years and years of work, sacrifice and all the hopes of a proud mechanized people.

Volan, seeing his dream fade, goes up to the top of the tower, overwhelmed with anguish and with death as his sole desire. He collapses due to grief. After a few moments he suddenly gets up, as if struck by a vision. His face shows great bewilderment. The man has been transfigured. No. He must not die, he must live to free Raun from being enslaved by Machines. And now Sacar, the queen of Raun, appears, in whose honor the tower of Raun was being built. Defying danger, she has come up to the summit in order to take stock of the situation and to question Volan about everything he plans to do to save the construction. To her great surprise, she no longer finds in him the man he was before, who she secretly loved, but a different spirit, a complete stranger to the world of machines. All of Sacar's words are in vain: Volan wants to demolish the tower. Not even the revelation of her great love for him can pull the Great Initiate back from his unshakable decision.

Due to the strange and incomprehensible language that Volan uses, Sacar comes to the conclusion that he must have gone mad and so she asks Sillan for help. All the incitements and prayers of his beloved disciple are in vain. Volan's only response is to command that the demolition work begins immediately. The loudspeakers issue the tragic news. All of Raun is in turmoil. The ergons, incited by Sillan, who sees everything as lost, rebel. Regarding Volan as the betrayer of their work, they take over the entire edifice and ascend the tower en masse in order to deliver justice. Their anger is without limits. Not even the queen's authority is able to pacify them. Four ergons seize Volan, who has now resigned himself to his fate, and are about to cast him into the void.

In the midst of this turmoil, the voice of the *Loudspeaker* announces that the Red Man, the Despot, is coming to pass judgment. Everything stops as if by magic. The crowd gathers together religiously. The Red Man, the purest heir of the mechanized race, the God of Raun, appears. He orders for the disobedient ergons to be immediately thrown from the tower. Then, turning to Volan, sternly, but at the same time with loving respect, he asks him the reasons for his inexplicable confusion. Volan replies boldly. But Sacar, whose love for him has grown even stronger, steps in to save him:

Volan must not be listened to. He is insane. His every word confirms this.

The Red Man decides to have Volan sent to the *Electric Prison*, where the seeds of his humanitarian insanity might perhaps be destroyed. Sillan is proclaimed the continuator of Volan's work. While Raun is rejoicing and on the tower Sillan is being cheered, the Loudspeaker warns that the tower is about to collapse. Everyone runs to safety. Ropes are thrown from a number of airplanes, to rescue those on the top. A clanging of metal, a terrible crash. Screams. Moans. The part of the tower that was in danger has collapsed.

PART II.

Volan is in the electric prison. Under the influence of electricity, he is delirious. Terrible visions laugh in his mind. He believes himself to be the absolute master of Raun and sees himself standing with the splendid Sacar at the top of the tower, now completed, while he receives tributes from his subjects.

From time to time his eyes appear animated but then immediately grow dull. He falls back into annihilation. The *Choir* invokes Divine Electricity to save Volan and bring him back to Raun.

In Volan's subconscious stream men and projects float, wrapped in a thick haze which from time to time is penetrated by flashes which reveal his previous life. In Imperial Rome he was the architect Aterius, builder of the Temple of the Sun God. At night, illuminated by thousands of swaying torches, he directs the arduous work of the slaves.

Just then, Sacar, who has covertly come to see him, enters. Volan does not see her as Sacar, but as the Roman courtesan Calpurnia, his lover. He calls her to him.

A scene from his previous life is recalled: invisible to Sacar, dressed in the garb of an ancient Roman, the ghost of the *Architect*, who was killed by Calpurnia due to jealousy, while he was building the temple, appears. Here, Sacar (Calpurnia) personifies Evil and the Architect, now that he is pure spirit, wants to free the earth from this poisonous plant, which has tenaciously taken root for the destruction of humanity. He comes near Sacar and wishes to strangle her.

A piercing scream. The scene darkens. Sacar turns off the electricity of the electric prison. The ghost of the Architect disappears. Volan is free. Sacar, feeling she is going to lose Volan for good, plays her last card, by revealing to him a plot she has hatched to kill the Red Man and take over Raun. Volan simply needs to agree to it. Everything has been prepared. But Volan disdainfully rejects this heinous proposal. He cannot feel any love whatsoever for a female like Sacar and he prefers to go back to the electric prison.

Sacar is desperate. Totally distraught, the only thing left for her to do is to distance Volan from her for good, relegating him to an island at the antipodes of Raun. Maybe then she will be able to forget about him.

Volan realizes that everything is lost. Once gone from Raun, he will not be able to accomplish his mission of redeeming the world from the machines. He is already "human". Nothing now ties him to the mechanical world. But maybe he can give life to a being who, born from a "humanized" father, would one day save a humanity otherwise inexorably condemned.

At night, with extraordinary audacity and in disguise, he risks penetrating the inviolable *Gynaeceums*, where the Virgins of Raun are kept under guard. He enters into the first cell that he comes across. Inside, the virgin Saib is sleeping, naked. He gently wakes her up, and takes the insensate girl into his arms. The womb of this automaton of flesh will give birth to a new being who will no longer be a machine!

PART III.

Raun has succeeded in completely mechanizing the individual and all of Earth, first by completely destroying family and human sentiments, and secondly by radically transforming sexual interactions. The genius of the Great Initiates has thus been able to create the *Gynaemachine*, which is the selector of the race and the most venerated idol.

The Virgins of Raun are kept inside the *Gynaeceums*, sacred and inviolable. No man, not even the Despot of Raun, can cross the threshold. By means of television cameras, they are kept under surveillance by the Sexual Service Department, which day and night keeps track of their monotonous lives and is ever-ready to fiercely punish the smallest failings.

Religious celebrations take place every year, which Sacar, the sovereign of all the females of Raun, attends. The Gynaemachine inspects the virgins who have reached puberty and divides them into three different categories. The attributes to gain access to each specific category are checked by the Gynaemachine with absolute precision. The virgins that have to be examined are called forward by the *Man-Number*. Under the surveillance of *Ber*, First Superintendent of the Sex Department, like stiff automatons they enter the Gynaemachine and, after a few moments, they exit with the appearance of the life for which they have been destined.

The Gynaemachine assigns the females destined for procreation to the First Category (M.). They are only allowed to have contact with the *Breeders*, those men who have been rigorously screened since childhood and who are specialized for this service. The sexual encounter is reduced to a simple mechanical function. Though nature has even given animals special times for amorous struggles and communications, these are denied to the people of Raun.

Mating occurs and is organized in such a way that the two beings can neither see nor speak to each other, thus preventing any passionate or sentimental exchange. Children, as soon as they are born, are immediately taken away from their mothers, who will never be able to see them again, and are raised in special establishments.

The females assigned to the Second Category (P.) are those destined for the pleasure of the Initiates — the intellectual and governing body of Raun — while the ergons, who are man-machines, are denied any kind of sexual encounter, which, moreover, would be inconceivable. These females are all infertile and remain in service for 10 years. Once this period has elapsed, having become useless, they are cast into blast furnaces.

The females assigned to the Third Category (L.) are female-ergons. They are beings without sex or instinct.

Their lives are solely dedicated to work. They are inter-mingled with the male-ergons, with whom no apparent distinction exists. With them, there is nothing but a work community. The senses are dead.

Raun has thus been able to transform nature and human instincts. In Part III. we witness one of these sacred annual celebrations. Sacar invokes the Sun and the Moon, which she considers herself to be the daughter of. The Choir sings for the happiness of the young ladies who are called on to live the beauty of a machine life.

Ber, the First Superintendent, presents his report to Sacar and energetically criticises Raun's system of life, saying that even though for hundreds of years it has performed smoothly and succeeded in mechanizing men as intended, in the long run it could be fatal to the existence of the populace.

First of all, the breeders are becoming increasingly more feminine and are beginning to lose their masculine traits. The Gynaemachine assigns almost 75 per cent of all virgins to Category P., thus creating enormous gaps in the other two categories, which are the most important and vital.

Furthermore, category P., despite the brief lives of its females, has become so large that it is seriously distracting the Initiates, whose efficiency, already the object of many studies, has started to diminish considerably.

The Gynaemachine has begun giving out its sacred results for class 328, and the results are negative for categories M. and L.

The loudspeaker announces that Sillan has come to pay an urgent visit to Sacar. Everyone leaves. Sillan, who has the grave task of continuing and completing the construction of the tower of Raun, already foresees the failure of his undertaking.

This gigantic task requires an enormous amount of human material. The supply of ergons has already been grievously eaten into. A few more years and he will be alone on the unfinished tower.

There is only one solution: to do away with the Gynaemachine so that all females can be mothers. Without doubt this would create substantial disturbances in the life of Raun, but it is the only way to complete the tower. Sacar protests against these absurd demands, as they would mean the end of Raun, and she wishes to punish the sacrilege. Sillan remains adamant. He sees nothing but a single reality: the tower. Sacar has one last weapon to win over Sillan: the offer of her own beautiful and unique body. And the ambitious Sillan, who wanted to bring to ruin his teacher Volan by abandoning him to the anger of the ergons, gives in.

The inspection is resumed, with the next category. The Red Man orders that a mechanism in the Gynaemachine be modified. Its functional ability is switched from 100 per cent to 80. So that the Gynaemachine will be lenient!

While a maiden is being inspected, the Gynaemachine stops. The signalization screen shuts off. Astonishment and anxiety. Everyone is shocked. A terrible disaster weighs on Raun. A female exits the Gynaemachine. An underhand anger explodes. Everybody wants to kill her, but Ber manages to control the enraged crowd.

The loudspeaker announces that the Red Man wants to question her. His word is law. Everybody leaves the scene. Only Saib remains, in front of the loudspeaker. The scene darkens. Reflectors project green light on the loudspeaker, which little by little gains in intensity until the loudspeaker's tragic character can be seen.

The Supreme Judge of Raun — the all-seeing Red Man — knows what happened, but all the same wants to interrogate the female Saib, and asks her who the man was who made her a mother. Saib vaguely recalls her adventure with the unknown person, who she never again saw. What wrong has she done? Was she not an automaton? Was she aware of herself and was she conscious of her action?

Her innocence is obvious and transparent. The Red Man, an inflexible but fair judge, cannot condemn her to death. He will forever ostracize her from the life of Raun by sending her far away. Saib begs to have her son with her. But the judge, seeing in the child, conceived by two "humanized" beings, the greatest danger to machine civilization, instructs that he be killed. As soon as he announces his decision, Saib faints and falls to the ground.

PART IV.

Volan has returned to the state of primitive man. Exiled to an island, in him there is but one desire: to escape and return to Raun. But how? He does not have any safe means of transportation at his disposal. Desperate, and even understanding that he will likely meet death, he decides to make a canoe from a tree trunk.

Meanwhile, from Raun, without a precise destination, an airplane departs on board of which is Saib, who must be sent away from the Empire of the Red Man. During the flight, the radio announcement finally arrives: "By order of the Supreme Judge of Raun, the female Saib has to be taken to island N. W. 1185 and left there. From Raun, the airplane must first go to island W. N. W. 421 and check if there are any signs of life from the ex-initiate Volan, etc. etc."

Volan hears the sound of engines. His joy is great. The plane veers and swerves down. It is clearly trying to land. Volan feels that it is bringing him life! Suddenly, a huge flame flashes through the sky. Two parachutes open. The plane has caught fire and crashes on the shore.

He runs like a madman so that he can offer help. Coming to the beach, he sees a woman dragging an inanimate body from the waves. He casts himself into the ocean and together they bring the *Captain* onto the beach, seriously burnt and almost dead.

Volan asks him questions and finds out that he comes from Raun. He does not want to give any information about the woman. On the contrary, he begs him to kill her. It is this that is his mission. The dying Captain insists, but Volan refuses. Faithful to the order received, the Captain gathers his last energy and throws himself at the woman, but falls to the ground dead.

At this point, the *Two Air Mechanics* arrive, whose lives were saved thanks to the parachutes. Volan gives them the task of throwing the dead body of the Captain into the sea. From the woman he learns that she too was exiled from Raun and her entire story.

They look at each other in silence. A great emotion has left them speechless. Then they embrace. They have recognized each other! Now Fate has reunited them again, now they can live happily, far away from the Devouring Metropolis. But Volan, more than ever before, feels the need to return to Raun in order to accomplish his mission.

Some of plane's papers, which were saved by the two air mechanics, give Sillan more precise information on the island's location. They try to save everything they can from the plane wreckage so that they can use it to make a boat that is less primitive and safer. Luckily, they find an undamaged radio device. Volan has a brilliant idea: he contacts Raun and asks for help using the identity of the two air mechanics. A radio communication from Raun asks news of the ex-Initiate Volan, who should be on that very island; Volan replies that there is an abandoned hut but no living soul has been seen. Volan must be dead.

The airplane has already left Raun. From the air mechanics, Volan gets the flying outfits, which he and Saib put on. He then orders the air mechanics to hide in the deepest recesses of the forest. Volan and Saib, dressed as air mechanics, become automatons of Raun.

PART V.

Several years have passed. Sillan, with unprecedented sacrifices and decimating millions of ergons, has succeeded in completing the construction of the tower. Thus, for the men of Raun, the Earth has become quite small. It is necessary that they hurl themselves towards the conquest of the planets. Sillan launches the first sideroship, which takes the first bold group of Earth's last inhabitants to Mars. The first interplanetary communications have been established.

The scene of Part V. takes place in the *Transplanetary Dockyard*, where the second sideroship is ready to be launched, which will carry the Red Man, Sacar, Sillan and the Great Initiates to take possession of planet Mars. Among those working in the dockyard are Volan and Saib, disguised as ergons. Volan uses the opportunity of this interplanetary flight to liberate Raun from its ferocious despots. The people, left without leaders, once they have got over their initial confusion, will have to follow him.

Volan, the great connoisseur of the loving heart of machines, easily understands all the secrets of the construction and propulsion of the sideroships. He, precisely calculating the velocity of the sideroship in space, is able to secretly tamper with the mechanisms that controls it. The sideroship will not be able to reach Mars and its entire crew is condemned to death.

The moment of the launch nears. The entire dockyard is rejoicing. The Red Man arrives with Sacar, accompanied by the Great Initiates. The Red Man delivers via radio his greetings to the first inhabitants of Mars and starts to board the sideroship.

The ergons who have built the sideroship want the honor of joining the Red Man, but there is only space for a very few of them. Sacar passes them in review in order to reward some with her choice. At a certain point she becomes pale and cannot help but let out a cry. It seems that, among the ergons, she has recognized someone. She immediately regains control over her emotions. Five ergons are chosen. The passengers board the ship. The sirens wail. There is a great roar, followed by a piercing whistle. The earth shakes. The sideroship is launched into space to the accompaniment of a thunderous ovation of enthusiasm. The loudspeakers communicate to Raun the various phases of the venturesome voyage.

While Volan and Saib listen with anxiety to the messages, Sacar, who, having been held back at the last minute by a mysterious force, had never left, runs toward Volan. She throws her arms around his neck and asks him how is it that he is still alive, how is it that she finds him there in the dockyard. Now, finally, Volan is hers: the antennas on the Tower of Raun will send into space the news of his return. All of Raun will salute the penitent Volan who has returned to the life of machines.

But Volan's words make it clear that he is now completely alien to Sacar and Raun. Just then, the loudspeaker announces the mournful message: "The sideroship, having been launched at a greater than planned velocity, which was impossible to adjust, has surpassed Mars' orbit without being able to enter it. Now it is drifting aimlessly in space. All is lost!"

Sacar understands immediately that this is the work of Volan, now understands that she has fallen into his hands and that she, from sovereign, will become slave. She flees to the top of the tower and speaks to her people. Defeated by her great love, she announces that Volan is now the leader of Raun and that everybody must show him obedience. She then kills her inner drama by throwing herself off the tower.

PART VI.

The exodus has begun. Volan orders the people of Raun to abandon the Metropolis. All the flying machines are used to transport what remains of the proud mechanical race to distant shores.

It is difficult, almost impossible, for the people to adapt themselves to the primordial fonts of life: agriculture and fishing. Nobody knows what to do, where to begin. Despite the regained freedom, there is general dissatisfaction. In the end, why was Raun abandoned? Humanity, without any longer having a soul, passions, love, what can it gain by returning to a primitive way of life, a life that no one knows how to live or can live?

On the beach the arrival of the air fleet bringing the last remaining men of Raun is anxiously awaited. Now Raun is deserted. Everything has stopped. The Metropolis is dead.

In the forest, which extends as far as the beach, a *Girl* is imploring a *Young Man*, who wants to be present for the arrival of the air fleet, to stay with her instead. The naïve words of the young man make it seem as if he is still living like an automaton, dazzled by the beauty of the life of Raun. He is oblivious to everything that could be called sentiment and instinct.

The Girl wants to be a representative of Nature which, despite having been violated and overwhelmed by the will of man, always keeps within itself the seeds of rebirth. With the same violence, with the same greed and implacability, Nature takes back its rights. And so it is that the Girl brutally reawakens the sexual instincts in the young automaton, crying out her desire for maternity. And so love is reborn.

The air fleet arrives. The exodus is complete. The people of Raun are free in a free land.

Despite many fanatics disagreeing, all the machines, piled on the beach, are blown up with dynamite. It is Volan, the apostle of the new humanity, who pushes the detonator button. The people of Raun do not wish to retain even a memory of them.

On a new earth, a new life begins. The era of machines has ended. Humanity journeys forth once more.

THE END